At last Adam stood up, uncurling his long legs from beneath her visitor's armchair, so that when he gazed down at her from his great height she felt dwarfed and at a disadvantage, so she too rose gracefully, her blue eyes hesitant in response to his dark, magnetic appraisal of her.

'Have a good weekend, Joanna,' he said softly. 'Let yourself go a bit, give something to the world, and you'll be surprised what you might get in return.'

After watching him stride away she sat down heavily in her chair again. Now what on earth was that supposed to mean? Didn't she give enough of her time and effort to the world as it was? The job she did with such undivided attention was surely giving something to the world! She held her head in her hands, suddenly lacking confidence and wishing . . . Dear God, if only she could turn the clock back and shut out the black memories which taunted her still, even after all these years . . .

Helen Upshall lives in Bournemouth with her husband, now retired. When quite young she became interested in Doctor Nurse stories, reading her much older sister's magazine serials instead of getting on with the dusting, so it was a natural progression to go into nursing in the late 1940s. Since she took up writing, ideas have come from a variety of sources—personal experiences of relatives and friends, and documentaries on television.

Love is the Cure is Helen Upshall's eleventh Doctor Nurse Romance. Recent titles include *Doctor From The Past*, *Sister Stephanie's Ward* and *New England Nurse*.

LOVE IS THE CURE

BY

HELEN UPSHALL

MILLS & BOON LIMITED
ETON HOUSE   18-24 PARADISE ROAD
RICHMOND   SURREY   TW9 1SR

*First published in Great Britain 1988
by Mills & Boon Limited*

© Helen Upshall 1988

*Australian copyright 1988
Philippine copyright 1988
This edition 1988*

ISBN 0 263 76258 0

*Set in Plantin 10 on 10 pt.
03-8811-57943*

Typeset in Great Britain by JCL Graphics, Bristol

Made and printed in Great Britain

CHAPTER ONE

JOANNA walked through the long corridors with Roxanne and her mother. Emerging out into the brilliant sunshine of a summer's day, she smiled at the young girl by her side. 'Let's hope it's a day like this in August when you walk down the aisle, Roxanne,' she said.

'Wouldn't it be lovely? Oh, it's too much to hope for—and that my scars will be faded by then.'

The long blonde hair of Roxanne's wig arranged to cascade down over one side of her face covered the ugly red weals of which Joanna knew she was conscious.

'Every week will make a difference now,' she assured the young patient. 'You'll be too busy preparing for the wedding to think about it. Won't she, Mrs Parkes?'

Roxanne's mother was a fashionable woman, full of self-confidence usually, but today she looked paler than normal and her eyes had lost the sparkle she endeavoured to reveal when visiting Roxanne.

'There's an awful lot to do,' she said wearily, 'but I expect we shall be ready. Somehow everyone is on the day.'

Roxanne's eyes had flitted across the large gravel driveway to where a sports-car had just pulled in. 'Oh look, here's Mr Royston. Now I can say goodbye to him.'

'But, darling,' her mother said quickly, 'you've got to come back to see him in two week's time.'

But Roxanne was already running across the path to greet the tall, handsome doctor. He pulled himself out of the low car and stood up, glancing round quickly to see who was approaching. They were too far away for their voices to be heard distinctly, but he was bending slightly to speak to Roxanne before he retrieved his briefcase from the back seat. Joanna inaudibly sighed with relief that he was managing to smile at Roxanne. He wasn't the easiest of men, yet she felt certain that he wouldn't deliberately shun anyone. Roxanne was hopping from one foot to the other, smiling up at him and talking eagerly.

'She's quite besotted with the man, you know, Sister Morris,' Mrs Parkes said impatiently. 'She's far too young to be getting married. I'm sure she doesn't feel as potty about Martyn as she does about Mr Royston.'

Joanna laughed. 'That's just infatuation, everyone feels the same, especially about a doctor who's so dedicated to his work and cares so much for his patients, whatever age they may be.'

'I've been too afraid to ask before, Sister, but Roxanne is going to be all right eventually, isn't she?'

'I'm sure Mr Royston will have told you that there's bound to be some permanent scarring, Mrs Parkes. Roxanne has done remarkably well in a very short time, you know.'

'Don't say that, my dear, you make me feel so guilty. It was all my fault, I shouldn't have gone off for the day leaving Roxanne to cook the dinner. It isn't that she's stupid, but she's never had to do things about the house before. I should have made sure she was capable.'

'If it's any consolation, Mrs Parkes, chip-pans overheating are the most common cause of accidents in the home, according to the Fire Service's statistics. In a way it was lucky Roxanne had such a lot of hair, that will grow again, but it probably prevented worse facial damage. She's going to look *so* beautiful on the day. I hope she'll come along to the ward when she comes in to Outpatients to remind me of the date. I'd hate to miss it.'

Mr Royston had his arm around Roxanne's shoulder as they came across the driveway, and as they neared Joanna and Mrs Parkes he looked up and acknowledged them with a rare smile. 'Mrs Parkes, Sister,' he said coolly, 'so we're going to lose our blonde bombshell today, then?'

'And I'm sure you won't be sorry, Mr Royston,' Mrs Parkes replied. 'At least it means a spare bed for someone else.'

'No doubt Sister here will be pleased to hear that, but we've quite enough patients to be going on with at present and not enough time to give them our fullest attention.'

'I can't tell you how grateful we are, Mr Royston.'

'Mr Royston has promised to come to my wedding, Mum,' Roxanne said excitedly. 'So don't forget to put him on the list.'

Mrs Parkes looked decidedly ill at ease. 'You mustn't be a nuisance, dear,' she said. 'I'm sure Mr Royston has a full diary.'

'Not necessarily for social occasions, and if I can possibly keep that day free I'll most certainly do so. Let me know as soon as you can. If you can't find me let Sister Morris know.'

'I shall see you at Outpatients' Clinic,' Roxanne reminded him.'

'You may see my Registrar instead of me, Roxanne, but you know Dr West very well and he knows your case.'

Roxanne was suitably quietened and Joanna felt a wee bit piqued with Adam Royston for being so unfeeling. But that was how the system worked. Roxanne's skin grafts had been successful, though her left ear still looked a mess underneath the hair, but now she could be dealt with by Julian West in Outpatients. Mrs Parkes took Roxanne's arm and led her towards the sunset red Ford Orion which was parked nearby.

'Take care now, Roxanne,' Joanna said. 'We'll see you soon.' She stood for a moment waving her off, and to her surprise Adam Royston waited with her.

'Let's hope Roxanne doesn't want to feed her new husband too many chips after they're married,' Adam said with a grin.

'I should think she's had enough of chips to last her a long time, but she isn't likely to make the same mistake again. She's going to look lovely in white, don't you think?'

'Yes, she's a very attractive young lady. She's lucky to have got away without worse injury. Make-up and her hair when it grows longer will help to hide the scars which I can do nothing about.'

'You could have seen her at your clinic, next time, surely?' Joanna questioned, then at his icy silence wished she hadn't voiced her opinion.

They had reached the door of Ampfield Burns Unit and Adam stood back to allow Joanna to enter first. She dared to look into his eyes, into an expression which told her in no uncertain terms that her question was out of order, but after walking a pace or two he stopped. 'Would I have made anyone else a special case, Joanna? Are you suggesting that Julian isn't efficient enough to continue with Roxanne's treatment?'

'You know I wasn't implying that. It's just that Mrs Parkes feels so guilty, and Roxanne wants to invite you to the wedding, so it would just have been a nice gesture on your part, I thought.'

'I do have a great many patients on my mind, Joanna, and there's more admitted every day, as you well know, so I simply cannot make Roxanne a special case, just because you feel that I should make a gesture of familiarity. By now, Joanna, you should know me better than that.'

Joanna sighed impatiently. Adam Royston was such a prig when he chose to be, which didn't endear him to the staff in general, even if he was admired for his skill. 'Sorry I spoke,' she said, in what should have been a humble apology but smacked of sarcasm. She turned to go back towards the floor where she was Sister-in-Charge. It was a post she hadn't long accepted, but she had been at Ampfield Burns Unit for three years now, first as staff nurse, then as Junior Sister on Children's Ward, and now she was in charge of the first floor where casualties and admittances came after initial treatment downstairs. As in most hospitals, though, staff were expected to go wherever they were most needed, and Joanna was no exception even though she was a Sister. The unit was quite small, the staff like one big happy family, a team united in helping the patients who came into their care. Joanna went straight to her desk and sat down to bury her head over some paperwork to hide her flushed cheeks, but almost at once her friend Lynn Dalton came on to the nurses' station.

'The ambulance has just rushed a family of five in, Joanna,' she said. 'Be prepared—I don't know all the details, but I believe there are two smallish children not too badly burned, so they may come up to the wards quite soon.'

'Can you cope down there—I could spare half an hour or so before we start teas?'

'I think we're OK, actually. Mr Royston has just come in, so we should be able to manage, but I'll soon buzz you if we can't.'

Joanna completed the page of her report which she was writing and then went to find her staff nurse.

'Mary, possibility of two beds on Children's Ward wanted shortly. Get teas started here while I go and warn them, can you?'

'Sure,' Mary said, and Joanna went along the corridor to a twelve-bedded ward where several of the children making good recoveries were seated at a table with a voluntary teacher. The rattle of the tea-trolley could be heard approaching, so Joanna looked around at the beds situation. As she went to speak to the toddlers confined to their cots, Angie, the nurse on duty, joined her. 'That's an ominous sign, Sister. You look as if you're trying to decide who to move?'

Joanna laughed. 'Something like that. As yet we don't know the extent of their injuries, but Lynn has just informed me that a family of five has been brought in, and two children might be transferred up here fairly soon.'

'Oh, dear.' Angie looked round at the young patients. 'A bit difficult at present as we don't know whether they'll want beds or cots, but we can move Matthew over to the other side and fit one more in next to the empty cot. I'll ring down for Dennis to come and give us a hand.' She disappeared into the office and Joanna went to have a word with eight-year-old Matthew.

'We're going to move you over to the other side, Matthew,' she said gently. 'How would you like to be next to David? He comes over to talk to you sometimes, doesn't he? You'll be up and about soon, I expect.'

Matthew looked at Joanna with wide questioning eyes. He was a quiet, sensitive boy who said little but watched intently all that was going on around him. He had been badly affected by dense smoke when a faulty electrical fitting had resulted in an electric blanket catching fire and setting the house ablaze before it was discovered. Fortunately Matthew was asleep at the time in a room where the door was firmly closed and the firemen had rescued him through the upstairs window. His father had pushed his mother and an elder sister to safety outside before going back upstairs to try to get Matthew out himself and in consequence had suffered severe burns to his face, chest and arms. He was still in a critical condition, and Joanna knew that Matthew had nothing to do except worry about his father. They tried to keep his mind occupied with different things, persuading the other children who were not confined to bed to talk to him, and cheer him up, but they soon gave up when they got no response. He still had trouble breathing, and was likely to for months to come.

'You'll like it next to David,' Joanna said cheerfully. 'He'll keep you amused if nothing else, and you can tell me in the morning if he snores.'

David came to seem what was going on, insisting on helping Dennis, the porter, who came to move the beds around.

'Will Matthew soon be able to get up and play with us?' he asked.

'I don't see why not,' Joanna replied. 'He won't be able to chase around because it hurts him to breathe, but tomorrow he can sit out in a chair on the balcony.'

Joanna wanted nothing more than to see Matthew joining in the activity in the ward. Lots of the children came in with horrifying burns and scalds, and one wondered if they would ever get over the shock, let alone the actual injury, but Joanna had found during her nursing career that children were the most resilient of patients, and showed a great will to fight for survival. The beds had been prepared for the new admittances, and teas cleared away before they arrived. Dennis brought a five-year-old boy, Anthony, on a trolley, and a nurse from Casualty carried the eighteen-month-old baby girl, Susie. 'A bed and a cot required,

Sister,' the nurse said as she put the child in Joanna's arms.

'We must be psychic, that's exactly what we've prepared. Put the folders on my desk, please, Nurse. How's everything going down there—having problems?'

'A whole family of five. These two are the least injured, but the others are all going into Intensive Care. Dr West is coming up to see you about these two later on.'

The children were put to bed side by side and a nurse was asked to special them until Joanna had read the report on them. As with Matthew, they were both suffering from the effects of shock, and inhaling smoke and fumes from an exploding gas boiler. Anthony also had a suspected fractured arm from being thrown across the room. They had been treated for shock in Casualty, Anthony's arm strapped up until he could be X-rayed, and now they were sleepy from the effects of the sedative they had been given. Joanna gave some instructions to the staff nurse on duty and then went back to the nurses' station to write up her report. She had been working there for about twenty minutes when the door opened and a tall, good-looking man came hurrying through.

'Hi, Joey,' he said affectionately. 'How are the two Malvin children?'

'Hullo, Julian. Asleep, I believe, poor little mites. Yet another gas boiler,' she added pointedly. 'How about the rest of the family?'

'Too early to say as yet, but all fairly serious. The boy you've got—um, Anthony, isn't it?—he's down for X-ray first thing tomorrow morning. Can you deal with that?'

'Yes, of course. Anything else?'

'Mmm—meet you for supper in the canteen? Unless you're going to invite me home?'

Joanna looked up at him with a wry smile. 'It's our night for going into Tullbury to help with the flower carpet in the Cathedral. You could always come and help if you like.'

Julian West made a face and turned to go, then changed his mind.

'Flower carpet?' he echoed, mystified. 'In the Cathedral? What's that in aid of?'

'To raise funds for the repairs on the Cathedral spire, of course. Don't tell me you hadn't heard, Julian? I know you're pretty heathen, but I thought everyone knew that the Cathedral spire is in danger of collapsing. Don't forget it's all very old and needs constant maintenance.'

'And I give generously when I'm asked,' Julian said indignantly. 'You said "we"—who have you roped in to help?'

'Lynn. We thought we'd do a section of the flower carpet on behalf of the hospital, but anyone can come and help.'

'Never heard of a flower carpet,' Julian said with doubt written across his face.

'You must have heard of flower festivals—churches have them all the time. The Cathedral is so large and high and ornate that it lends itself to being decorated with flowers, and the carpet will be made up of flowerheads stretching through the centre aisle. It should look lovely.'

'I'm sure you'll do your bit admirably, Joey, but I don't think I'd be much help. Looks like I'll have to eat alone again.'

'You're a permanent guest at my cottage, so stop feeling so sorry for yourself, but actually we're going to have supper in the canteen before we go into Tullbury,' Joanna said.

'What time?' he asked.

'In about an hour's time, if I can get away.'

'Mm, don't know whether I can wait that long, and as you're going on into Tullbury maybe I'll make do with eating at home for tonight. Take care, and don't stay out too late.' Julian gave her a friendly pat on her back and hurried off. Joanna watched him go with a fond smile on her face. Everyone thought, imagined that she and Julian were into a serious affair. On some days she thought so too, but then he would make some remark just as he had done now about her 'taking care' and she'd realise that he was more of a protector than lover. They had their moments, quite intimate ones sometimes, when maybe they had been to a concert or show, with supper at her cottage afterwards. But that was good food and wine taking effect; by morning she, and she suspected Julian, was glad that they had exercised self-control before becoming too committed. She loved him very dearly, but not always in the way she felt would be right to last a lifetime—well, not as man and wife. He did protect her, sometimes too fiercely, in an old-fashioned gallant way which could be embarrassing. His possessiveness sprang from their having met first as doctor and patient, though that was their secret, and the result was that other eligible men steered clear of her. Julian was a useful friend to have because he cared so much for her welfare, but there were times when she could well do without his monopoly. He had a lively personality which coincided with his boyish appearance, and his mousy-coloured hair was in complete contrast to Adam Royston's dark, brooding good looks, even though they were about equal in height of six feet, give or take a centimetre or two. Their characters were in contrast too, Julian the lighthearted man about town, while Adam, although only two years his senior, was highly qualified, and dedicated to his profession, with little patience or time for fun and frolics of any kind.

Joanna sighed, wondering why on earth her thoughts should turn so readily to the senior surgeon when she herself was out of the running for any man. Maybe it was envy after hearing so much about Roxanne's plans to have a lovely white wedding in Tullbury Cathedral in a few months' time. And thinking about the Cathedral made her hurry up to complete her report so that she could get off duty.

After handing over to the night nurse Joanna went to find her friend, who was already in the canteen.

'Nothing very special on the menu tonight,' Lynn said dispassionately. 'I think I'll settle for a salad as we shall have a fair bit of bending to do later on.'

'You sound like some matriarch who's got to consider her hiatus hernia,' Joanna laughed.

'After a day like today I feel like some ancient matriarch,' Lynn responded dismally.

'Come on, cheer up, you'll feel better when we get outside the hospital.'

'Hospitals and churches aren't the type of places that make me feel on top of the world somehow.'

'You are in the doldrums—you seemed all right earlier, what's happened to change things?'

Lynn, a pretty, golden-haired girl of twenty-four and a year younger than Joanna, pouted slightly. 'Oh, nothing—just got on the wrong side of Sir when we had the family in. Just a conflict of ideas, nothing serious—he just makes me feel totally inadequate.'

'I know exactly what you mean—but we should know him well enough to know how difficult he can be. Young Roxanne has been discharged today and she wants to invite Adam to the wedding.'

'Whew, poor kid, I bet that didn't go down very well.'

'Actually he was quite nice about it and said he'd go if he possibly can, but when I suggested that he could see her at her next appointment in Outpatients he said he couldn't make her a special case and that Julian is quite capable of checking her condition. Poor Roxanne was quite put out about it, I think. Her mother said she's potty about Adam, much more so than with the man she's going to marry.'

'Sounds as if she's a bit young to be getting married.'

'She's a young nineteen, very indulged, and yes, I agree that she probably is too young to be settling down. Unfortunately it will no doubt turn out to be one of those marriages that will only last a year or two.'

'Now who sounds in the doldrums?' Lynn said. 'Trouble is we're getting on and no prospects. Don't know about you, but I feel hopelessly depressed sometimes. Much as I love my job I would much prefer to have a future as a wife and mother.'

Joanna fell silent as she picked up a ham salad from the shelf and took it along to the end of the counter to pay for it. She followed Lynn to a vacant table and they sat down to eat. 'I'm quite happy with my life as it is. I don't think I want to give up nursing yet awhile.'

'It's all right for you, you keep poor old Julian on a string and he'll be happy to wait until you decide the right time has come.'

'It isn't quite like that, Lynn,' Joanna said solemnly. 'I know everyone takes it for granted that we're—well, you know, but we're not that close. We both know that we're free to go our own way at any time.'

Lynn snorted in disgust. 'Hm,' she said, 'it doesn't look like that to me. He's besotted with you.'

'It may look like that, but you're quite wrong, in fact I can't imagine us being any different from the way we are now. We certainly never discuss the future, we're just good pals.'

Lynn snorted again, unconvinced, but both girls concentrated on eating rather than discuss their private lives, and when they had finished they put on light jackets over their uniforms and went outside to the declining sunset. It was still early summer and the evenings were inclined to be chilly. They walked to the staff car-park where Joanna's white beetle stood waiting. Seat-belts fastened, it rumbled into life and Joanna drove the three miles into the heart of the city where the Cathedral was situated, its tall significant spire reaching up towards the heavens.

The girls shivered as they went inside, but it was peaceful, and they gasped in admiration of the array of flowers gathered in various pots and vases awaiting their destiny to be part of the long carpet through the main aisle.

Mrs Stenning-Young came to greet the girls. 'It really is most kind of you to come to help us,' she greeted effusively. 'You all work so hard at Ampfield and you must get very tired.' She directed Joanna and Lynn to the part of the carpet which they were to design and left them to it.

'They haven't given us a very large section,' Joanna grumbled. 'S'pose they didn't think we were up to it.'

'I hope you've got some ideas, because this isn't my scene really. I'm not artistic,' Lynn said with some doubt about the task in hand.

'I thought we could make a lovely flame-coloured background with a white bird and a blue one on it—symbol of peace, and also patriotic in red, white and blue?'

'Very inventive,' Lynn agreed, and they went in search of the flowers they needed.

In hushed tones they worked out the pattern and were spacing out the birds when Joanna noticed a pair of largish feet close by. She looked up and found Adam Royston watching them. By his expression she guessed that he was not particularly impressed.

'Hullo,' she said in a whisper. 'Have you come to help?'

'I thought it was my duty to put in an appearance, but,' he shook his head from side to side negatively, 'I'm not too sure I can be of much use with that?'

'Oh?' Joanna sat back on her heels. 'You—er—don't think much of it?'

'I'm sure you have excellent reasons for being patriotic, but a red background? Blue bird? A *dove*?' Each word held more emphasis, emphasis of despair.

'We're open to suggestions, maybe you'd like to do it?' Lynn suggested.

His face lit up, he took off his jacket and threw it on to the nearest pew, then knelt beside the girls.

'I thought——' he began, then realising his mistake corrected it to: 'May I suggest that you choose something slightly less fiery? I know we deal with burns, but—' he looked directly into Joanna's blue eyes and smiled quite wickedly for him, 'we should depict gentleness, healing, sympathy, don't you think?'

Lynn stood up as if she intended to leave there and then, and Joanna frowned at her, begging her to stay. 'How on earth can you depict feelings in a carpet of flowers?' Lynn snapped.

'Ah, a good question—Lynn.' By using her Christian name Adam was placating her, obviously. 'The artistic impression, you see, my dear. Pale yellow for gentleness, wouldn't you say? With a touch of white for purity?'

'Colourless.' Lynn's tone was less than congenial.

'We must use some bright colours, surely, Adam?' Joanna questioned politely.

'Yes, blend them in gradually, weave your emotions into the pattern—like life.'

'No birds?' Joanna asked.

Adam gazed into her eyes and held her question in abeyance as if he wouldn't offend her by his reply.

'Butterfly, perhaps,' he said, raising his eyebrows.

'Angels' wings would be better,' Lynn commented cryptically. 'Nearer to Heaven in here, I suppose.'

If looks could kill! Joanna thought, but she simply began arranging some greenery round the edges as Adam stood up and went to fetch more flowers.

'You're making a good job of antagonising him,' Joanna said to Lynn frantically.

'So what's he doing interfering anyway?'

'Search me, but he is hospital staff, I suppose.'

'But this was supposed to be *our* effort, yours and mine. You didn't have to invite him along.'

'Hey, wait a minute,' Joanna said. 'I didn't invite him.' She was thoughtful for a few seconds before she said, 'I did suggest that Julian might like to come along—maybe he told Adam.' She shrugged, and at that moment Adam returned.

'I hope you don't think I'm interfering,' he said, smiling down at Joanna and turning on Lynn forcefully. They didn't reply. It was apparent to them that he knew exactly what they were thinking, but it soon became apparent that he also knew something about design and colour. Lynn stood and watched while Joanna simply did as she was told, then suddenly Lynn said: 'I think I'm surplus to requirements here, so as I'm tired I'll go on home now.'

Joanna stood up quickly. 'I'll run you home,' she offered.

'No, don't bother, it's only a five-minute walk from here—see you tomorrow.'

Adam didn't bother to look up or say anything until Joanna knelt beside him again. 'Bit touchy, is she? Did I put paid to her ideas?'

'No, they were mine, actually.'

He paused, long enough to gaze at her again with his earnest, genius eyes.

'Sorry—it was a bit garish, I thought, not really like you.'

'It wasn't supposed to be like me,' she said, 'and I do think it needs more colour.'

'Whatever we do, my dear Joanna, is a reflection of our inner self. You don't strike me as being a conspicuously colourful character. Now let's see . . .'

Joanna felt as if she would burst with indignation, but she managed to curb her temper and watched silently as he created a beautiful design using colours from the palest yellow to deepest bronze, then adding a highlight of burgundy red. No birds or butterflies, she noticed, just an intricate mosaic of colour, and she felt humiliated that he had done something so tasteful. He had just added the final touches when Mrs Stenning-Young came up.

'Adam, my dear, we're all going now—oh, how absolutely perfect, how clever you are! The verger will want to lock up. Are you coming in for coffee?'

'Er—I ought to see Joanna home.'

'There's no need. I've got my own car,' Joanna said, now feeling much as Lynn had done—surplus to requirements.

'I'm going in that direction anyway, so can I beg a lift?' Adam asked.

'You won't be calling in to see your father, then?'

'Not this evening. You go on, just tell Peter that we're still here. I must make absolutely sure . . .' He began fiddling with his arrangement. Was he deliberately delaying having to escort Mrs Stenning-Young? The older woman thanked Joanna for 'doing her bit' and went off with some other ladies. Adam stood up and stretched. 'Thanks for the rescue—but I do need a lift.'

'But you don't know——'

'Milton Lane, isn't it? That pretty little place down towards the stream?'

'That's right, but how did you know?'

'Julian mentioned visiting you one night after we'd been operating late. He worries about you, being on your own, so the least I can do is to make sure you get home safely.'

'Haven't you got your own car?'

'No, I walked in.'

'But you can't live as far out of Tullbury as I do?' Joanna insisted.

'Trying to get rid of me?'

'No, but you don't really need a lift, do you?'

'I guess I could manage, but I am gasping for a cup of coffee. Besides, I'd like to see this hideaway cottage of yours.'

'And how are you going to get back again?'

'Walk, I expect, but that's not your worry. Shall we go, then?'

They paused to take a last look at Adam's handiwork which Joanna had to admit did look very effective, then they went out into the darkness of the car-park. Joanna was lost for words, she didn't imagine that Adam Royston was used to travelling in an old beetle, a far cry from his impressive sports job, but he seemed quite happy to get into the passenger seat beside her.

There wasn't much traffic and once past the gyratory system the country road leading towards Ampfield was almost deserted. A right-hand turn and up the hill, then down into the valley and another right-hand turn off into a very narrow lane where there were no street lights, and there nestling among conifer trees was her cottage.

The outside light had come on automatically at dusk and she brought the car to a halt at the front door. The cottage was old but had been renovated and completely modernised inside, which evidently came as something of a surprise to Adam. He stood looking up at the roof, walked round the side of the cottage to the garden and came back with his hands in his pockets, deep in thought.

'Tell me how you came by this cottage?' he asked, coming into the kitchen where she was switching on the coffee pot. He'd have to do with heated up coffee at this time of night, she had no intention of making fresh. She poured some milk into a saucepan and put it on the electric stove.

'I got it through an agent. It had been empty for some time. I wanted to buy it, but I couldn't get a big mortgage on such an old place, so I offered to pay half of the improvements.'

'And the owners agreed?'

Joanna laughed cynically. 'You bet—they were pleased to have someone take the responsibility, but Julian made sure that the agents got their half in advance before the work was started.'

'But that means that you've had to take out a mortgage for

the modernisation and you now pay rent as well?'

Joanna was reluctant to divulge too much about her private means, but Adam Royston was the senior surgeon, and he was known for being a kind of godfather to all the younger staff.

'I had a decent sum of money in the bank,' she said slowly, 'and I did need a place of my own rather urgently when I came to Ampfield.'

'Good heavens, girl, surely you could have had a room at the hospital?'

'When I came three years ago I was a staff nurse and would have had to share.'

'So? You must have shared numerous times before during your training?'

Damn the man! Joanna felt herself going trembly. He was getting too inquisitive.

'I preferred to have my own room, and when that wasn't possible I tried to get a flat, but they're like gold-dust, the only ones available were on the other side of Tullbury. The idea of an isolated cottage appealed to me, and I'm very happy here.'

'Not an ideal situation, and you should have been persuaded not to embark on such a deal.'

'It's all legal,' Joanna assured him hurriedly. 'My brother came down from London and checked that everything was in order.'

'What about your parents?'

'My father works in the Foreign office and they're in America. They like it there, so they'll stay even when he retires.'

'So you're quite independent?'

'I like it that way, I've had plenty of practice. I've been on my own since I was seventeen.'

'And you're now——'

'Twenty-five.' Cheek, she thought. It was none of his business how old she was. 'Come through into the lounge,' she invited as she poured the coffee into the two cups she had put on a tray along with a plate of biscuits. He allowed her to lead the way and she was aware of him going to the patio doors and looking out on to the back garden. Thank goodness she had mowed the huge lawn and weeded the flower borders.

'Someone likes gardening,' Adam observed.

'I don't mind,' she said, 'and someone has to do it. As I live alone it has to be me.' She hoped she was sounding positive. He turned and sat down on the cottage suite settee. It was covered with beige-coloured material with a design of huge flowers, mostly pinks and mauves, which matched her décor of shell pink walls and heavy velvet curtains in deep dusky pink. The carpet wsa also pink with a white squiggly pattern all over it, bringing life to the room as a whole.

'I like your decoration and furnishings,' Adam complimented with a wry smile, and she knew he was trying to hide his surprise after the suggested design for the flower carpet. 'You've had two rooms knocked into one, but most satisfactorily, if I may say so. Even the wooden beams across the ceiling matching up.'

'I had a good builder and decorator, thanks to Julian.'

'Ah yes, Julian. You shared his flat at one time, I recall—when you first arrived at Ampfield?'

'Julian and I knew each other before that, he's been a good friend to me, but I wish people would stop marrying us off. He had room in his flat for me to sleep on the couch, until this cottage was ready—nothing at all scandalous about our relationship.'

Adam held his hands up in surrender and laughed. 'OK, a taboo subject, but he thinks the world of you, and he's a nice man and an excellent doctor.'

'I couldn't agree more.'

He sipped his coffee thoughtfully, and ate three biscuits, while Joanna wished he would hurry up and go away. But he had something on his mind. Was he going to stay long enough to divulge what it was, or was she going to be left in suspense?

'I find it rather surprising that a young woman likes living alone in quite such an isolated spot—but then you would appear to be an enigmatic young lady.'

'I most certainly am not, there's no mystery about me, Adam,' she said in self-defence.

He inclined his head and gazed at her as if trying to break through this barrier of quiet reserve of hers which he had become so much more aware of lately. Or was it that he just hadn't noticed too much about the personalities of his staff until now? He knew they called him the Godfather, but that was only because he liked to show concern for any of the younger members of the Burns Unit. Treating patients whose bodies were badly injured and disfigured needed a special kind of understanding, and he knew how the young nurses agonised over children in particular. Dealing with the relatives of such patients also required sympathy and a barrel-load of patience. Was Joanna finding the job more difficult than she had anticipated? Or was her reserve becoming more prominent because of this lonely existence of hers? Then again, she might not be as lonely as he imagined—there was Julian, he remembered.

'What sort of agreement do you have with these agents, then, Joanna?' he asked.

'The usual kind of thing, if and when I leave the cottage the owners will reimburse my half of the modernisation costs if the property has been kept in good repair.'

'And what length of lease do you have?'

'Three years, it's coming up for renewal shortly.'

Adam drank his third cup of coffee, then stood up to leave.

'I'd better run you home,' Joanna said. 'I don't know how far——'

'Within walking distance, Joanna. You've been most kind, though I still feel you shouldn't be living in this particular spot alone. Surely as you have a spare room it would be economical to have a paying guest?'

'I suppose it would—but sharing presents all kinds of problems and when I've finished work I like to come home and be able to please myself what music I listen to, what telly I watch, whether I eat or not, whether I go out or stay in—I've been alone too long now to want to change.'

He patted her arm gently, said goodnight and went off with what Joanna considered was a disapproving expression. She closed the front door, then leaned her back against it as the awful truth dawned on her. Was he angling to share?—or worse still, did he want her out so that he could rent or buy the cottage himself?

CHAPTER TWO

JOANNA'S night was a disturbed one, yet she was too troubled and tired to get out her fire-proof personal file and look up the actual date on which the renewal date was due. It was June now—yes, she had come to Ampfield three years ago in March, but had stayed at Julian's flat for nearly four months while all the work was being done, which meant that her lease would be up in a month's time. Adam Royston's interest must have some bearing on that. But why? She knew that he already had a very nice country home himself, though she wasn't quite sure where. Perhaps he only rented his house and was due to have to leave and look for something else. Willow-Weed Cottage was situated just the right distance from the Burns Unit. It suited Joanna very well, so would be equally convenient for Adam. She hoped she was wrong, she hoped that he wasn't going to ask her if he could share the cottage, and she went on duty the next morning with some trepidation, but when they passed in one of the long corridors he simply smiled in his own inimitable way and greeted her as if they were almost strangers.

The pandemonium of the children's ward did nothing to help her confused state of mind. Susie had been fretful all night and refused to sleep, setting up a howl when her brother Anthony had to go to the X-ray department. In the end Joanna had to take Susie too, and afterwards they watched while he had his fractured arm set in plaster. Anthony was in some pain and needed rest, but the only way he got it was when Joanna agreed to let Susie lie in his good arm, and soon they were both fast asleep.

Joanna must have appeared quite flushed by the time she reached the canteen for her mid-morning break. She asked for tea and a cheese roll and then went to where Lynn was waiting for her.

'I thought I'd have to go back on duty without seeing you. Thought maybe our Adam had eloped with you.'

'You must be joking—but I believe he wants me out of Willow-Weed Cottage so that he can have it for himself.' Joanna gave her friend all the details and then agreed that it did sound as if she had let her imagination get the better of her.

'He's got a super house up on the hill. I'm told that it's large, standing in acres of ground with a high wall surrounding it and well guarded against intruders with a massive German shepherd dog on patrol. He lives alone, why shouldn't you? You haven't any cause to suppose they won't renew your lease, have you?' Lynn asked.

'No. I've kept up my rent, and payments on the loan. I didn't tell Adam that I've paid that off, and now if I had the chance to buy the cottage I could probably get a good mortgage, especially as I've been promoted since I took it over. That's what I wanted to do, buy it in the first place so that I could really call the place my own, but it wasn't possible then. I was hoping that I could make an offer now when the time comes.'

'So what's stopping you? Just because Sir is showing an interest and seems concerned about you living alone down a country lane it doesn't mean that you can't still do it.' Joanna was grateful for Lynn's confidence, the one thing she lacked in her own personal life.

'I suppose so, but he was too interested, too nosey, Lynn. He was prying, and for a special reason—I only wish I knew what it was. He said that it was Julian who told him where I lived, casually, when they were working late one evening, which doesn't really warrant all the interest. Besides, he was quietly examining all the alterations and would have loved me to invite him to see upstairs, but I didn't. It was rather late, after all.'

'Your friend Julian has got some explaining to do,' Lynn said. 'First he tells his boss that we're helping with the flower carpet, which seems to have given him the right to take over, and now he's sharing personal confidences. Mm, I'm not too sure that I like that. I didn't think your Julian was a creep.'

'Oh, Lynn, he's not. I'm sure he hasn't told Adam anything that he considered was confidential. People do talk, and often let things slip without thinking. Anyway, you're coming to the Sunday morning service, aren't you?'

'No.' Joanna almost jumped at the positive refusal. 'Sorry, Joey, but I told you churches aren't my scene. I'm fond of flowers, it seems awful to me that people will walk all over that lovely carpet on Sunday. I only agreed to help because we're friends and I like to help in worthy causes. I like the idea of the flower festival very much, but seeing all the flowerheads pulled about made me feel quite sad. I'm not an atheist, or agnostic, in fact I think I'm quite religious in my own way, but when you see patients brought in with such dreadful injuries, children so horribly burned, I begin to question my faith.'

Joanna was thoughtful for several minutes. 'I know what you mean,' she agreed slowly. 'But we must have something to believe in, and man is cruel, to say the least. When we . . . people . . . face death, they frequently find that their faith is the strongest. I suppose it's natural to clutch at straws. A dying man, even an atheist, invariably cries out to his God to save him in a desperate situation. I honestly couldn't do the job I'm doing if I didn't believe in a life hereafter and a loving God. We tend our patients, doctors do a marvellous job with skin grafts and plastic surgery, but most of them would admit that there has to be some divine intervention in the biggest majority of successful cases.'

'Listening to you makes me feel such a heel for doubting, Joey. No wonder the patients all love you so much. You have a caring nature, but you also have a reason to care, and that's what makes the difference. Still, I hope I'm learning from folk like you, and Adam and Julian, then when you and Julian go off and get hitched I shall be in the running for your job.'

'So that's the reason for you trying to get me to the altar—bet you beat me to it, you're prettier than me—and younger.'

'Come off it—only a year, and Julian won't let you escape his net, I'm sure.'

Joanna sighed. 'I wish you'd realise that there's nothing serious between us, Lynn. We're fond of each other, but not enough for marriage—and anyway, I'm not the marrying sort.'

'I wouldn't make any rash bets on it if I were you. You aren't too upset about me not going to church on Sunday, are you? Mum will expect me to stay in and watch TV with her. Fat chance I've got of ever meeting any nice eligible men—still, I can dream.'

'I'm sure your mother would like nothing better than for you to have plenty of dates. She's so nice, Lynn, and you're nice too for showing her that you care, but she must realise that you have a life of your own. After all, she won't always be around. You weren't at the last hospital dance, so you'll never meet anyone new if you stay at home.'

Lynn stood up, and at that minute a beseeching voice on the intercom asked that Sister Morris should return to her floor at once. Joanna also stood up and in a second had left the canteen, leaving no one in any doubts about her priorities. When she reached her office she was surprised to see Adam Royston waiting for her, and he didn't look in the best of tempers.

'Ah, Sister,' he said shortly, 'Mr King's condition appears to be deteriorating, so I'd like to try an experiment. Could you take Matthew up to Intensive Care and sit with him and his father for a few minutes, just talking—you know the drill, we've had failures and successes in the past so we've nothing to lose in this case. I wanted Matthew to see his father before this, but I had to be sure the boy wouldn't be too shocked. Matthew himself is withdrawn, so maybe this will help them both, what do you think?'

'It's difficult to tell, as you say, we can get so little out of Matthew, but it's worth a try. I had the idea on my mind but thought perhaps it would be best when his mother and sister visit.'

'Then why the hell didn't you speak up and say what you thought?' Adam questioned angrily. 'You must learn to communicate, Joanna, don't keep all these little gems to yourself. You're with the patients a great deal more than Julian or myself, it's what we expect of you, that's why you're in charge of this floor. Unfortunately time may be running out for Mr King, so we can't wait until Mrs King gets here. Go and prepare the boy now, then bring him up when you think, *if* you think he can take it.'

Joanna wasn't at all sure that Matthew could take this added strain, but she went to his bed where he was propped up by numerous pillows, supposedly reading, but she knew that he had chosen the book several days earlier and had not advanced beyond the fifth page.

'Hullo, Matthew, how do you feel today?' she asked kindly, taking his hand in hers. It felt cold and clammy, and instantly his breathing began to labour as he eyed her suspiciously. 'I suppose you'll have some visitors later on today?'

'Will my dad come?' he asked in a husky voice.

'Your dad is here all the time, Matthew, but he's rather poorly. How about you visiting him?'

'I could? You mean I can get up and go to his ward?'

'Would you like to?' Joanna asked with a hesitant smile. She knew that Matthew wanted nothing more than to see his father, but what did he expect? 'He isn't at all well, Matthew, can you be very brave?'

'Is he? . . . Will he look all black and burnt?'

'No, darling, but he will be covered with lots of bandages, and he may look as if he doesn't hear you, but I'm sure he'll recognise your voice. Just come with me and we'll have a peep at him. He may be asleep, of course, but if you don't want to stay you don't have to, all right?'

Matthew nodded and pushed back the bedclothes eagerly. His small unhappy face was ghostly white and had been ever since his arrival four days earlier. Joanna's heart ached for him, knowing the anguish he felt at the uncertainty of what had happened to his father. Bit by bit they had tried to explain to him what had occurred on that fateful night, tried desperately to find out what he remembered of the event, but he had clammed up and refused to talk about it even to his mother and sister. It was early days yet, but Joanna knew that the time had come when different tactics had to be tried. She couldn't tell an eight-year-old that his father's condition was giving cause for concern, she just had to pray that hearing his son's voice might give Mr King something to fight for. No one knew what might be going on in an unconscious patient's brain. It was possible that the poor man thought Matthew had been dead when brought out of the burning house. He had rushed back inside with no consideration for his own safety, not realising that the firemen were reaching Matthew's room from outside. Joanna experienced an involuntary shiver. The sight of a burning building was one you never forgot. The smell of smoke lived with you for months, the fear for those in danger, the panic when trapped, seeming flames licking round windows and doors getting closer and more fierce. Sightseers gathered quickly, taking pleasure, it seemed, in morbid tragedy. She hated seeing films on television which showed these things, yet she wondered if it might help people to be more aware of being careless with cigarettes and matches, faulty appliances, electrical wiring, if they were constantly reminded of such dangers. She let Matthew put on his own slippers and get his dressing-gown out of his locker, not because she wouldn't help, but it was important to persuade him to help himself. She did tie his belt, and then with his hand in hers she took him along to the lift. The Sister-in-Charge of Intensive Care greeted Matthew with a smile, the kind of smile which disguised her intense concern for the man in her charge.

'So you're Matthew,' she said cheerily. 'Your dad is asleep, but if you'd like to sit by his bed and talk to him he might wake up.'

Matthew's eyes surveyed her critically but he said nothing. Joanna felt his grip on her hand tighten, so she guided him forward and Sister Audrey Garrett took them along to where Mr King's bed was hidden behind screens. Joanna paused at the foot of the bed, allowing the little boy to take in the scene without pushing him too far. If he wanted to run then Joanna would be right there to run with him, because she knew the felling all too well. But after a few seconds while he became accustomed to the silent reverence of the ward, which was quite different from the children's ward, he pulled his hand free and went to his father's bedside. It seemed as if he completely forgot that anyone else was there as he gently laid a hand on his father's arm.

'Dad,' he whispered, 'Dad, it's me, Matthew—I'm all right,

you can wake up now.'

Joanna looked at Audrey and without a word both girls left the room, Joanna returned to her floor, and Audrey to watch from her office window. On the way down the stairs, which Joanna decided to use instead of waiting for the lift which seemed to be delayed, probably due to another patient being brought in, she met Julian.

'Ah, there you are, Joey. Thought you must have gone off duty without telling me.'

'No, I'm on until four o'clock, and off until Monday morning.'

'Any plans?'

'Church on Sunday morning.'

'Oh yes, how did the flower arranging go?'

'Thanks to you we didn't have to do it, and Lynn opted out halfway through.'

'How could Lynn opt out halfway through if you didn't have to do it?'

'Adam Royston gave us the benefit of his valuable assistance, in fact I suppose he really did the job all by himself.'

'He did? I didn't know he was into that kind of thing.'

'Neither did anyone else. It's done now, and as it's a special occasion I'd better go to support the Cathedral on Sunday.'

'Lynn going too?' Julian asked.

'No, she doesn't fancy seeing the flower carpet walked on.' Joanna smiled up at him. 'And you won't be there either.'

'Afraid not—on call, you see. Is something wrong, Joey? You look slightly put out.'

'I'm very put out, actually, Julian. Firstly you didn't have to tell Sir that we were doing a patch of the flower carpet. Lynn and I wanted to do it by ourselves, I only suggested you might like to come for company.'

'Now hold on a minute—I didn't even mention it to Adam. I had no reason to, and I certainly wouldn't have thought he would have been interested. Not guilty, Joey, and—secondly?'

'You told him where I live, and after finishing his expert design he had the cheek to ask for a lift home with the idea, it seems, of sussing out Willow-Weed. Could it be that he wants it for himself? You know I don't like everyone knowing my business.'

'Joey dear, you're jumping the gun at an alarming rate. You're way ahead of me. I haven't told him anything about your affairs, honestly, except that one evening when we were operating late I happened to mention that I'd intended to visit you. He asked where you lived and I told him, but no mention was made of your personal lifestyle, so why should he be interested? Besides, darling, he has a mansion of a place on the hill, so what would he want with charming little Willow-Weed?'

'Funny, that's what Lynn said, but his interest was too keen, more significant than the fact that I lived there.'

'You know the Godfather, he's afraid you're going to get into debt or something, perhaps.'

'Julian, I've lived there for nearly three years and he's never taken the slightest interest before. Doesn't it seem rather pointed to you that just when my lease is coming up for renewal in a month's time Sir was very keen to see inside?'

Julian grinned mischievously. 'You're only disappointed that he didn't make a pass at you—yes, that's it, he probably had such ideas, then decided he needed to melt you first. Better watch out, Joey, Adam always gets what he wants in the end, we all know that.'

Joanna all but stamped her foot angrily at Julian, and with a hiss of despair she turned and hurried down the remaining stairs to her floor where she sought sanctuary in her office. Trust Julian to make light of it! Everyone knew the woman who managed to inveigle her way into Adam Royston's affections would have to be very special indeed. It was Julian's last remark which worried Joanna—he did always manage to get exactly what he wanted, and she was convinced now that he wanted her cottage. Where on earth could she go? And how had he known about her going to Tullbury Cathedral? Even more important was how had he managed to find out about her agreement with the agents? Joanna sighed with dismay. She supposed he had lived in the area long enough to know the right kind of people who could be useful to him, but that still didn't explain why he would want the cottage when he had this marvellous place of his own. Maybe he was the one in debt, or had discovered that a large house could be a lonely place to return to after a hard day's work, and having visited the agents to put his property on the market he had somehow learned that Willow-Weed Cottage might be up for grabs. The agents must have got hold of the wrong end of the stick and for some reason were assuming that she did not want to renew her agreement. She cursed the fact that as it was the weekend they would be closed, but she resolved to make a call to them at the earliest opportunity.

For the next couple of hours she had little time to think about her own problems as the wards on her floor were kept busy with physiotherapists' visits, a continuous stream of patients being taken to and from the various clinics and the X-ray Department, so before she knew it the lunch trolley had arrived. Joanna gave a few instructions to her staff nurse, Mary, about diet before she returned to the Intensive Care Unit to fetch Matthew.

'Hi, Audrey, I've come to fetch my little boy. Any progress?'

Audrey Garrett shook her head. 'No response from Mr King, but perhaps Matthew can come back later when he's had a rest and his mother and sister come in. If they all sit around and talk it may stimulate Mr King. At least he's no worse, his condition has stabilised, thank goodness, so now we must persevere to try to bring him round.' She nodded to the view of young Matthew through the window. 'He's a nice little boy. Quite a big age difference between him and his sister. Eight, did you say? Victoria's fifteen, so I suppose Matthew has been doted on by all the family.'

'But he's certainly not spoilt. In fact he's sort of sad and lonely—oh, I know some of that is through these terrible circumstances, but I get the feeling that he was a bit withdrawn previously. Most children quickly get back to normal and take any injuries in their stride, but Matthew—well, it's almost as if he's blaming himself.'

'A chat to Mrs King might help,' Audrey suggested. 'We can't appear to be too inquisitive during the crisis stage, but now we've got to probe a bit in order to get some response from Mr King and help Matthew.'

'I'll try to have a chat with her before I go off duty, but I'm finishing at four o'clock until Monday. They need time, but we'll let Matthew come up here quite often now and by next week maybe things will look brighter for all the family. What about the Malvins?'

'Mrs Malvin isn't too bad, she's determined to improve for the sake of the two little ones you've got. The older girl, Elizabeth, seems to have come off worst because she was in direct proximity to the boiler in the kitchen, with Mr Malvin. The mother and two smaller children were sitting at the table having tea. I reckon, though, that both Mr and Mrs Malvin will be out of Intensive Care within forty-eight hours.'

'That's good news. Anthony and Susie are in shock and still very distressed, but apart from Anthony's broken arm their physical injuries aren't too serious. Poor kids, it must have been an awful shock for them.'

'Mrs Malvin told me that they'd had the boiler changed recently. Some cowboy knocking at the door asking for work hoodwinked them into believing he was a fully qualified plumber and central heating engineer. How vulnerable we all are—I get so sick of house pedlars trying to sell me insurance, double glazing, loft and cavity wall insulation, or this stone cladding, and not content with calling sometimes quite late in the evening, they've now taken to trying to get us by telephone.' Audrey grumbled, but goodnaturedly.

'I don't get many callers, thank goodness, being in such an isolated spot, but I've had one or two telephone calls—and not all nice enquiries, but I keep my whistle handy,' Joanna laughed.

'I can't understand why you live alone,' Audrey said. 'I thought you and Julian would have shacked up together by now?'

'Not you too!' Joanna groaned. 'Hospitals are notorious places where you're robbed of privacy—I'm desperately trying to preserve mine.'

Audrey raised her eyebrows. 'I couldn't wait to have someone share all my expenses and worries—there's nothing like the institution of marriage, Joanna, I can thoroughly recommend it, but then I'm biased, having a lovely guy like

Chris to look after me.'

'But you still go on working,' Joanna noted.

'Mm—well, Chris's job isn't that safe, whose is these days? But in a year or two we hope to start a family. Mortgages are crippling, aren't they?'

'I had a loan, the cottage was too old and run down for me to get a mortgage, but I'm hoping when the lease comes up for renewal in a month's time that they'll agree to sell to me.'

'Who owns Willow-Weed?'

'Some wealthy Joe Bloggs who didn't need it so let it deteriorate. When housing is so short there should be a law against people who allow their property to fall into disrepair.'

'It's all right now, though, isn't it?'

'Super, I'm really pleased with it. You and Chris must come over for a meal or a barbecue before the summer's out,' Joanna suggested.

'We'd love to. Better make it soon before they turf you out. You know what landlords and agents are like, now that you've done all the hard work they'll be able to get a good price for it.'

'I'm going to do my damnedest to buy it myself, and I have to say they've been fair up to now.' But Joanna stored away in her mind such worries as being turned out once the lease ran out. Audrey had voiced suspicions that were already there, but which Joanna had so far refused to consider, but now that Adam Royston was being unduly inquisitive she began to feel that her worst fears were about to be realised.

She went with Audrey into the ward, where Matthew was sitting by his father's bedside clutching a seemingly lifeless hand.

'It's time for lunch now, Matthew,' Joanna said softly. 'Perhaps you'd like to come back when your mum comes in later on?'

The little boy gazed up at Joanna with trust in his expression, and even the hint of a smile. 'Can I?' he asked. It seemed as if he had to question everything, as if he didn't truly believe anything anyone told him.

'Of course,' Joanna said. 'I'm sure your dad knows you're here, but he's weary and needs a good rest for the moment.' Matthew stood up and allowed himself to be drawn away, and once back in the children's ward he sat happily at the centre table with the other children who were not confinded to bed-rest. David greeted him enthusiastically.

'Shall we have a game of draughts after dinner?' he asked.

Joanna watched as Matthew shook his head. 'I'm going back to sit with my dad,' he said proudly. 'He's unconscious, so I've got to help him wake up.'

Joanna smiled at Mary. At least Matthew was talking, and his knowledge of the situation was surprising.

After lunch Adam and Julian with a group of student doctors came to do the rounds, and Adam was pleased to hear that Matthew had responded to the idea of sitting with his father. 'We must be careful not to overdo it. We don't want the boy to think he must keep vigil, but a short while here and there and then bringing him back to be among the other youngsters should be remedial for him,' he said hopefully. Joanna walked along by his side, passing him the relevant notes as they came to each patient, and when he had seen all the children they went to the other wards on that floor. Finally they ended up in Joanna's office to discuss the different cases, their treatment, and welfare, about which Adam was renowned for being most meticulous. When he passed the last file of notes to Joanna he dismissed his team with a few minor instructions and then smiled at Joanna.

'I'm sure you were about to offer me a nice cup of tea,' he said.

'Against the rules, except for medicinal purposes,' she said impishly. She didn't know why she was being nice to him when he was about to oust her from her home, but she couldn't help but admire Adam Royston, and her reactions to him were not always quite what she intended.

'And for consultants in need,' he added.

'It is rather warm today,' she said, 'and promises to be for the weekend.'

'And you're off duty, I understand?'

'Yes. Time to sit in my lovely garden.'

'Alone?'

'Most likely. What better way to relax?'

'Hm . . . not good for the mind, my dear. You need a

companion, someone energetic and frivolous to get you out of
yourself. Help you to forget the responsibilities of your work.'

'It's for that reason that I like my own company. I expect I
shall see Julian,' she added, then wished she hadn't. Wasn't
she trying to impress on people that there was nothing serious
in their relationship? Assuming in such a matter-of-fact way
that she was sure of seeing Julian hardly verified her denial of
anything intimate between them.

'I'm giving an 'at home' barbecue evening next weekend,'
Adam said, 'but I suppose you'll be on duty?'

'Yes, but I shall finish at six on Saturday evening,' she
explained.

'Splendid, I'm eager for you to meet a friend of mine. Will
you take that as an official invitation, then? You and Julian, of
course, and your friend Lynn, but I've already told her about
it, suggested she bring her mother too, it will make a nice
change for her. My swimming pool is heated, so bring your
bikini or whatever.'

Joanna felt herself go cold at the thought, but with a brave
smile she said: 'It would have to be a heatwave for me to find
enough courage to go swimming.'

'I'm sure we can find ways of making you enjoy yourself,
Joanna, so be prepared for a fun evening—no need to be
modest, leave that behind for the wards. By the way, I hope
you'll be attending one of the services tomorrow at the
Cathedral? I looked in this morning and the place is a blaze of
colour, the carpet is most attractive, but I feel I must apologise
for—well, taking you over, I suppose. Lynn was decidedly
displeased with me and quite heated at the thought of people
walking on the flowers, but once they're picked their life is
rather short, and it is a special occasion.'

'I can see Lynn's point of view, it does seem a bit
destructive, but as you say, it's only a one-off situation. The
cathedral is such a beautiful building, it lends itself to a flower
festival.'

She took care not to tell him which service she meant to
attend, and during the short time it took her to make the tea
and both of them to drink it they quickly reverted to topics
concerning the patients.

At last Adam stood up, uncurling his long legs from beneath her visitor's armchair, so that when he gazed down at her from his great height she felt dwarfed and at a disadvantage, so she too rose gracefully, her blue eyes hesitant in response to his dark, magnetic appraisal of her.

'Good,' he said in a self-satisfied manner, 'let's hope Matthew can strike a chord in his father's memory quite soon. Have a good weekend, Joanna let yourself go a bit, give something to the world, and you'll be surprised at what you might get in return.'

After watching him stride away she sat down heavily in her chair again. Now what on earth was that supposed to mean? Didn't she give enough of her time and effort to the world as it was? The job she did with such undivided attention was surely giving something to the world! She held her head in her hands, suddenly lacking confidence and wishing . . . Dear God, if only she could turn the clock back and shut out the black memories which taunted her still even after all these years. Memories of a tragedy followed by blank, meaningless days which time had eventually helped to fill to a certain degree, thanks to dear Julian whom she thought she loved implicitly, but now there were doubts even about that. There would always be a unique understanding between them, nothing could erase what had gone before, but now Joanna felt as if forces beyond her control were coming between them, altering the situation and causing her to feel nervous about the future. Had there ever been a future for the two of them? She had taken him for granted, and like most of her colleagues at Ampfield thought that one day she would be his bride and walk ceremoniously down the aisle of Tullbury Cathedral to stand proudly beside him. She tried to eject the visions which were superseding his image in that role. He had been her protector for too long, they had matured together in spite of his being her senior by seven years, and now she supposed they had become complacent about their situation yet aware of the fact that they must seek new adventures and friendships. Joanna sighed in despair. It was all right for Julian, he was attractive, lively and a fun person, he would have no difficulty in finding a new partner, but for her—what impossible dreams were to be her nightmare?

CHAPTER THREE

THE WEATHER remained hot and sunny, so Joanna went home that afternoon full of energy to do what little housework was necessary. She felt happier in the knowledge that young Matthew was at last making progress and coming out of himself, pleased that he was included in the family gathering which sat around Mr King's bedside hoping and praying for a miracle, and when Joanna went to church on Sunday morning she remembered that in her line of duty she witnessed many miracles, which gave her renewed hope. The Cathedral seemed exceptionally resplendent with the sun warming the cold stone walls and reflecting a kaleidoscope of colour from the masses of floral displays in every corner of the old building, which was filled to capacity, not only with local inhabitants and regular attenders but also many holidaymakers. Joanna took her place in a remote corner, hidden, as she preferred to be, by a large pillar which had been decorated with a variegated ivy intertwined with small white flowerheads. She was intrigued by the people coming in after her, calmed by the gentle music from the organ, and then her heart was stirred by a group of people taking their place to the right of the centre aisle. Adam Royston was following behind the dignitaries of the city, including Mrs Stenning-Young, who was well known for her work on the Council and among the less privileged. Joanna recalled that she seemed to know Adam rather well—perhaps there was a Miss Stenning-Young in whom he was interested—but then Joanna's attention was drawn to another family who were claiming their seats just in front of her, and as the attractive young girl glanced round she saw Joanna and acknowledged her with a smile and discreet wave. Joanna responded likewise to Roxanne, and thought again what a lovely girl she was. Mr and Mrs Parkes were with Roxanne, but there was no sign of the young man she was soon going to marry. Joanna's thoughts moved on to the arrival of the choir and clergy processing through the centre aisle on the impressive carpet of flowers, and she felt a certain sympathy with Lynn, who would have felt outraged at the desecration of God's handiwork even if she didn't believe in His existence. It was a lovely service, and as she returned to the warmth of the summer day outside she felt at peace, with a private contentment which she could find nowhere else but during and after a time of devotion. She supposed she wasn't natural to enjoy such inspirational gatherings and her own company. She couldn't explain it either, but that was the way she was made. No, not made, she reflected, rather conditioned to this kind of life, and she knew it was no use fighting it.

'Sister Morris, I knew you'd be here today. Doesn't the Cathedral look splendid? Mum said somebody ought to be married here while the arrangements look so fresh. I think someone may have been yesterday, because I can see traces of confetti.'

Roxanne had run to catch up with Joanna as she was leaving.

'It does look as if you're right, Roxanne. How are all your arrangements going? Couldn't you have brought your date forward?'

Roxanne sighed. "Fraid not. Poor old Marty has been sent to Saudi to work for three months, so it looks as if it'll have to be postponed until later in the year, and I did want a summer wedding.'

'Surely they would understand about his wedding?' Joanna questioned in surprise. 'Did he know about the possibility of going abroad?'

'Mm . . . sort of, but if you ask me, someone's got it in for us and is doing their best to put us off getting married at all.'

'Oh, I'm sure that can't be true, Roxanne. It'll work out all right, you'll see.' Joanna turned as Roxanne's parents joined them, and then Adam came hurrying towards them too.

'Good morning, everyone—beautiful day, and a most enjoyable service, didn't you think?'

Mr and Mrs Parkes agreed, and Joanna nodded when Adam

looked directly at her. He smiled down at Roxanne. 'And
how's our blonde bombshell, then?'

Roxanne fluttered her eyelashes at the handsome consultant
and snaked her body closer to his. 'I'm fine, Mr Royston. My
hair is growing fast now and I feel better every day.'

'Getting excited about the wedding, no doubt?' he asked.

Roxanne repeated her news, while Mr and Mrs Parkes
listened patiently, exchanging surreptitious meaningful looks,
which seemed to indicate to Joanna that they might have had
some hand in getting the wedding postponed. Joanna
understood their concern, Roxanne was young and immature,
but life was so uncertain, wouldn't it be better to let things take
their natural course, and accept any consequences? If Roxanne
found out she would lay the blame before them at every
available opportunity if things went wrong afterwards. Mrs
Stenning-Young came up then to claim Adam, so Joanna
slipped quietly away, to the car-park close by where she felt
more secure in her beetle, and homeward bound. After lunch,
which she ate on the patio in the sun, she wrote a letter to the
agents who handled the lease of Willow-Weed Cottage, then
she drove into the city and delivered it by hand so that they
would find it when they opened on Monday morning. She
explained about her promotion and said that she would like the
owners to give her first refusal if the option to buy the cottage
was still open. She felt certain that getting a mortgage would
be no problem now and decided to visit her insurance brokers
at the first opportunity. On her way home she paid a brief visit
to have a chat with Lynn's mother as Lynn was on duty, and
then she returned to the cottage to prepare tea for herself and
Julian. He arrived a little later than she anticipated, but he
explained that a patient had been admitted with bad facial
burns following the explosion of a picnic stove with an
incorrectly fitted cylinder.

'His hands are badly injured, but his sight will be the worst
worry. He's in Intensive Care, of course—but there's hopeful
news about Mr King. While young Matthew was sitting with
his father this morning he opened his eyes and smiled at his
son. He hasn't actually said anything yet, but every few
minutes he looks about as if trying to place his surroundings.

Naturally we aren't pressing him to speak, but as you can guess, Matthew is chattering nineteen to the dozen.'

'Miracles do happen, as I was reminded in church this morning,' Joanna said.

'And as you know from personal experience, Joey.'

She smiled appreciatively and they fell into a mellow silence, both of them grateful for the other's company and a chance to relax. But Joanna felt there were things hanging in the air which neither could bring themselves to discuss. It seemed that Julian was conscious of the atmosphere too and found a way to detract from it by suggesting that they went for a drive and drink somewhere, which pleased Joanna. They drove down to the coast and afterwards returned to their local inn where they met up with some of their colleagues, the topic of conversation being the forthcoming visit to Adam Royston's élite home and the barbecue.

'I suppose he'll engage a firm to do the catering,' someone suggested. 'Can't imagine him knowing what to do with sausages and beefburgers.'

'Don't you believe it,' Julian said shortly in his boss's defence. 'Adam is a very capable man. If he puts on a do—not that he does very often, but when he does he makes a superb job of it, and does the cooking himself. The swimming pool has to be seen to be believed.'

'And when did you see it?' Joanna asked, wondering why Julian had never mentioned it to her before.

'I had to go up there once to see him about a patient. He showed me round, but he did seem to live like a recluse then. Suddenly he's decided to live it up a little. I expect there's a woman around somewhere, maybe he's got married secretly and is going to introduce her to us next weekend. He's invited you, I take it?'

'Yes, but I don't have to go, do I?'

'Indeed you do—and why not? It's only courteous to accept such an invitation, Joey. He is our boss, and in a way I expect it's to show his appreciation for all we do.'

Joanna laughed scornfully. 'It's our job, Julian, why should he have to show any appreciation?'

'Because he's that type of man.'

'Oh, come off it. He's a most difficult type, and certainly not the sort you'd expect to invite his workmates home for a drink.' Joanna was thoughtful for a few minutes, then she said: 'But you could be right about the woman. He said he wanted me to meet a friend of his. He also said to bring my swimsuit, so that lets me out, doesn't it?'

'No, Joanna,' Julian said defensively. 'You've got a nice one-piece which reveals nothing, but does the heck of a lot for a man's imagination.'

Joanna laughed to hide her dismay. She hated being the object of criticism, and even the hint of admiration, but she supposed Julian was right, her one-piece was modest if nothing else, and that she meant to preserve at all costs in spite of Adam suggesting that she could leave it behind. He thought he knew everything about her when, in fact, he was ignorant of a great deal, which was how she wanted it to be.

It was quite late when Julian took Joanna back to Willow-Weed Cottage, and he went inside to ensure that everything was all right.

'You know, Adam was right to be concerned for you, stuck all out here in the middle of nowhere,' he said, glancing round at the neat orderliness of the place. 'You're on your own too much, Joey. It isn't good for you.'

Joanna turned on him, her face pale and stiff with emotion. 'You've been talking to him about me!' she accused with a hurt expression.

'No, darling, not in the way you think. You told me that he invited himself here and looked over the cottage.'

'Not all over it,' she denied hotly. 'I didn't invite him upstairs, but I couldn't help him seeing what he wanted to see down here. What is this—a campaign to get me out of the cottage? Why should he suddenly be so interested in where I live? It's never concerned him before, so it must be that he wants it for himself.'

'With that lovely mansion up on the hill? Wait till you see it, Joey. You'll adore it.'

'But if he thinks I'm lonely here what about his loneliness?'

'It's different for men—besides, he's got the dog, and you know what they say about dog being man's best friend. Not for me, I prefer female company. I can't say what's precipitated Adam's interest in you and your lifestyle. I can only assume that having seen where you live he doesn't think it's an ideal place.'

'Well, he'll have to think again, because I've delivered a letter to the agents in Tullbury, asking if I can buy Willow-Weed. It's my home, Julian, I love it here, and I like my own company. Don't forget the hours I put in at the hospital, and I'm not exactly alone there, so to be on my own here makes a pleasant change.'

'Maybe Adam hasn't reckoned with all the hosts of friends you've got.'

'Now you're being sarcastic, and that isn't like you. I haven't had to go searching for friends because you've always been around, and I'm grateful, but if you're trying to find a polite way of telling me you've had enough of being my guardian then that's fine by me. I've got Lynn and several of the other girls. It's better not to have friendships which are too demanding.'

Julian took her in his arms and kissed her roughly. 'Joey, you know I'll never have enough of you, but I think we both know that this isn't the kind of relationship which is going to lead anywhere. There was a time . . . but just lately I've felt things changing between us. You don't need me as your guardian any more, you can cope by yourself, but I'll always be here should you need anyone—you know that.'

Joanna sighed. 'I'm sorry, Julian, I understand what you're trying to say, and if you meet someone else I shall be very happy for you. I've been rather demanding over the past few years, haven't I? How selfish can you get? Of course you want your freedom, but we're colleagues and I hope we can remain friends?'

'Joey, now you're making a big issue out of it. Of course we're going to stay as friendly as we've ever been.' He grabbed her round the waist and squeezed. 'Who else would understand your hang-ups, for heaven's sake?'

'Now you make me sound as if I were due for the funny-farm. I thought I'd dispensed with all the hang-ups.'

Julian hugged her closely and kissed her again, but in a

brotherly way.

'I'm not too sure about you buying this old place, though,' he said thoughtfully. 'It will always need renovating, these ancient cottages do, if it isn't one thing it'll be another. OK, go ahead and renew the lease by all means, that's sensible, but borrowing a great deal of money to put into something as old as this needs some consideration.'

'You didn't think so when I first came to Ampfield,' she said, gazing up into his bright eyes.

'As I recall, darling, you didn't have much option. You were so against sharing in the nurses' home, and my flat wasn't really large enough for two—well, not in those circumstances, but maybe I was wrong, maybe . . . if I'd kept you there with me . . . I wonder what situation we'd find ourselves in by now?'

Joanna laughed, if only to relieve the tension. 'Probably have torn one another's eyes out by now! That's why I don't like sharing, Julian. Even with another girl. There's a lot to be said for independence and being able to please oneself.'

'As long as you don't become too dogmatic, too self-centred.'

'You don't think I am already, do you?'

'I think the same about you that I've always thought—that you're very sweet, attractive too, and I'm very fond of you—but —'

'But?' she prompted.

'We must be honest, Joey, time has changed us both. You especially—probably due to just the factor of your new-found independence. Something which I know you value, but don't let it dominate your life. Maybe that's what Adam can see which we never have before, that you've become obsessed with it.'

Joanna leaned back to look at him searchingly. 'You really think that?'

'No,' he sighed impatiently. 'I hadn't noticed anything except that we—well, maybe something was coming between us, and maybe, just maybe it's this independence of yours.'

'Then perhaps Adam has done us a favour by forcing us to stand back and look objectively at the situation. I admit that in the past I have depended very much upon you. I couldn't have managed without you, Julian, and I'm really grateful. I suppose I did think at one time that it was bound to lead to a more permanent relationship, but I don't think that either of us want that, do we?'

'I would have married you, Joey, if you really wanted that.'

Joanna's cheeks flushed to dark red. 'Don't be so patronising! Because you know a little more than most about me and the past you'd be willing to ruin both of our lives just because you think I expect it? Oh no, Julian. Surely we know each other well enough by now to be honest to a fault. You don't love me and I don't think I love you. Love grows, so they say, but in our case it's done the opposite. We've become too natural with each other to allow for growth of the sensational sort. It's better to admit it now, isn't it?'

'I didn't intend this to be a slanging match, Joey. It's late, and you're tired.'

'Of course I'm not. I've had the weekend off, remember? I'm glad we've had this conversation, it should clear the air and we both know now where we stand.'

'In exactly the same spot as before, my darling Joey. When you need an escort I'll be there, when I need a button sewn on I shall still come to you.' Julian laughed and soon had her laughing with him, but Joanna knew that they had been too honest for any further closeness to develop.

After Julian had left she wandered round her cottage, unable to settle to do anything. She felt confused, hurt even that such a conversation had been necessary, and yet knowing and liking Julian as much as she did realised that it was best to happen at this point. It didn't alter her position in respect of the cottage. She had made her own decision about wanting to buy it and she intended to stick to that. She was always grateful for Julian's advice and had been for the past seven or eight years, but now she was quite capable of managing her own life, and this was one decision she felt very positive about. Willow-Weed cottage was her hideaway, she needed it to be that way, and no one was going to persuade her otherwise. Somehow, though, the night brought a new loneliness she hadn't noticed before and she went on duty the next day feeling less than fresh, and easily irritated. But she was heartened by the change in Matthew, who greeted her eagerly.

'Dad woke up, Sister,' he said. 'He keeps looking round, but he doesn't say anything.'

'You'll have to be very patient, Matthew,' Joanna explained. 'Your father was quite badly burned, which will cause him a great deal of pain for quite a while, so we have to keep him sleepy until he begins to get better.'

'But I can still go to sit with him, can't I?'

'Of course, but we don't want you to get bored, so I think it's time you joined in with the lessons when Miss Bennett comes, then you can visit your dad after lunch.'

Matthew didn't look very pleased with that idea, but he didn't complain, and later on Joanna noticed that he was happily entering into all that the other children were doing round the big table in the middle of the schoolroom. Miss Bennett was a treasure, a woman in her mid-thirties who adored children and had a way of teaching and entertaining at the same time, and seldom had to admit defeat even with the most unco-operative child. The system wasn't designed to be of great academic value but rather to persuade children to forget whatever tragedy had resulted in them being a patient at Ampfield. They played word games, Monopoly, laughed through charades and quiz games, which all played a vital part in their rehabilitation. Miss Bennett's voice was almost never raised in anger and the children responded to her quiet supervision with a possessive love.

It was mid-afternoon when Adam Royston came through the swing doors with his usual flurry.

'Any problems?' he asked as Joanna picked up the pile of notes from her desk.

Joanna went through the list of names of patients whom she needed to report on or ask his advice about. They sauntered through the wards on the first floor while Adam chatted with each of the patients, paying special attention to those who needed extra reassurance.

'Where's young Matthew?' Adam asked.

'Upstairs with his father, where else?'

'Don't let him overdo it. Mr King is in a tremendous amount of pain and discomfort, so he's heavily sedated for the moment. I can't even be certain that as yet he's recognised that Matthew is all right. I know he wakes up from time to time, but he looks around in a daze. No doubt some of what Matthew and the rest of his family say to him registers, but it will be some days before we can make a reasonable appraisal of his condition.'

'Matthew seems to be enjoying his sessions with Miss Bennett at last. He didn't look too happy about it when I suggested it, but he's much more outgoing now.'

'Another conquest for you, Joanna, I knew you'd succeed in the end.'

'It was nothing I did. Visiting his father and his reaction is responsible. We can never be certain what goes on in these children's minds, but suddenly I notice that Matthew has very little trouble now with his breathing. How much longer do you think we need keep him in?'

'Mm . . . I'll examine him thoroughly in a day or two, but I'd rather he stays in until he can see some improvement in his father. Matthew is the baby of the family and his father dotes on him, according to Mrs King. He risked his own life to save Matthew when it would have been better to leave it to the experts.'

'That's an easy thing to say after the event, Adam. In that kind of situation you act with the urgency a fire demands. People are accused of panic, but what else do you do when someone you love is trapped helplessly inside a burning building? It's the same story which affects almost every patient in this hospital.' Joanna noticed the hint of a smile playing round the corners of Adam's mouth. She didn't consider she had said anything the least bit humorous and his reaction annoyed her. Then he handed back the file he had been looking at, and his smile generated a warm glow inside her.

'Evidently going to church yesterday aroused some emotions in you, Joanna. I was pleased to see you there. We had a good turn-out, didn't we?' What did you think of the festival in general?'

'Very impressive. It was nice to see Roxanne there too, but I have a nasty suspicion that her parents might be partly responsible for her fiancé's departure to Saudi Arabia—I can't think why they didn't choose the South Atlantic.'

'I wouldn't know, I'm not in their confidence, but I can appreciate their worries. Roxanne is a delightful youngster, but she has a lot of growing up to do still. Oh, by the way, Mrs Stenning-Young will probably be making her presence felt shortly by delivering and arranging lots of the flowers here at the hospital. The festival will be over tomorrow and then the floral displays are to be spread around to deserving causes in the area, and we're to be one of those.'

'I'm sure they'll be greatly appreciated, but we do get more than we can handle as it is.'

'Then take some home to that lovely cottage of yours. They won't last anywhere as well as they do in the Cathedral, as it's cool there. I only wish I could transport the floral carpet up to my house as it would brighten up the terrace for next weekend. Just pray for a good day, Joanna. The grounds are so spacious that it'll be a pity if bad weather forces us to go inside.'

'Wouldn't it be better to cancel if there's the likelihood of rain?'

'Not cancel, postpone perhaps, if we hear of a hurricane coming in our direction, but I don't give up easily and the forecast is good. So don't forget your swimsuit.'

Adam met her gaze intently and then left the ward. Joanna knew that he was due in theatre with some exacting skin grafting to do, which sometimes took several hours.

Anthony Malvin was in less pain now that his arm was properly set in plaster, and had begun to join in some of the activity in the ward when his baby sister would allow him to. She was quite fretful and as yet there was no sign of Mrs Malvin being well enough to be transferred to a small room, where she could look after Susie. A new extension had been built at Ampfield since Joanna had been there, which consisted of a floor of large rooms enabling families of varying numbers to be nursed together, which was ideal where there were small children needing to be near their mothers. Susie was frightened and difficult to console for much of the time, which was a strain on Anthony, but he never complained. Joanna and the nursing staff did their best to relieve him of the responsibility whenever they could, but Joanna was hopeful that Mrs Malvin would soon be out of Intensive Care. The effects of smoke and dust was not something which vanished after a few days' rest, it lasted for weeks, months, even years, but in the case of the exploding gas boiler there were other injuries as well as deep shock to be treated.

A few days passed without any further admittances to Joanna's floor, which gave her time to spend with the most poorly of her patients, while the staff, nurses and doctors alike became excited about the forthcoming Saturday evening at Adam's home. At first it was arranged that Joanna would take Lynn with her, but then Julian offered to take both girls in his car.

'Not that any of us are likely to get blotto, but in case Joey has one drink too many and gets over-excited she'd better not drive,' he said saucily.

'I think it would be better for me to drive,' Joanna insisted. 'It's you men who are likely to forget how many you've had.'

'Have you ever known me have too much to drink?'

'There's always a first time,' Joanna warned.

'Not on Saturday with two charming girls to look after.'

Joanna was quite pleased that Julian had offered to take her to the event. It meant that she had a ready-made partner, but when they reached Adam's luxurious house on the hill Adam himself came at once to claim her.

'Julian, take Lynn under your wing, there's plenty going on, some high jinks in the pool if you'd rather swim before you eat, and I want Joanna to meet a friend of mine.'

He hardly gave her time to breathe as he guided her into the house, and when they entered the huge sitting room a tall elegant woman stood to greet them. She was wearing a magnificent sari in turquoise and gold and with a flash of white teeth smiled at Joanna.

'So this is Joanna,' she said. 'I'm so pleased to meet you, Adam has told me so much about you.'

Joanna looked nonplussed. How could Adam tell this Indian woman anything about her when he knew nothing himself?

'Joanna, this is a doctor friend of mine, Kamla Ramarsingh. she's coming to Ampfield to join our team for one year and is looking for somewhere to live. I told her I knew just the person who would be glad to share her home. Willow-Weed cottage is quiet and not too far away from the hospital. Ideal for you to continue your studies, Kamla. Well, Joanna, what do you say?'

Joanna stared at him stupidly. What was there to say? Her head began to spin, her eyes became blurred and she was totally speechless.

CHAPTER FOUR

THE INDIAN woman smiled in sympathy.

'I must apologise, Joanna, I think this has come as a surprise to you,' she said kindly. 'I'm sure a room can be found for me in the hospital for the time being. Adam, I know you have my interest at heart, but you should have played this idea of yours a little more coolly.'

'But . . . but, Joanna?' His dark eyes glowered at Joanna, making her feel guilty, giving her cause to think that if she dared to oppose his suggestion—no, it wasn't that, she decided with annoyance, it was an arrangement he had already made. 'You have room,' he went on, 'and the cottage is much too isolated for you to live there totally alone. It's only for a year, and Kamla will be company for you.'

Joanna pulled herself up to her full height, gaining her composure with some difficulty. 'I don't mind living alone, in fact I prefer it,' she said. 'Nothing personal, Dr Ramarsingh, I hope you understand?'

'Of course, and it's Kamla. It's true I do need somewhere to live away from the hospital, so if you get any bright ideas perhaps you'll let me know?' Her smile was enchanting, her dark Asian eyes full of understanding, and Joanna felt a moment's pang of envy at the beauty of the woman. She had felt it in her bones that a woman was the cause of Adam's interest, but she hadn't anticipated this! Adam was all but breathing fire by her side, she could feel his anger, and although she felt inadequate to do combat she was determined to stick to her guns.

'I'm in the process of making an offer to buy my cottage,' she explained hesitantly. 'There'll be a lot to sort out during the next few weeks, and if they won't sell to me they may well turn me out when the lease expires.'

'Of course they won't, Joanna,' Adam cut in tetchily. 'I'm

sorry—I suppose I should have made it clear why I was interested in Willow-Weed. At least think it over—please.'

'I'm sorry, Adam, but my mind is made up—and how do you know that they won't turn me out?'

Adam scratched his head, his eyebrows raised significantly. 'Come on,' he said, suddenly grabbing her hand. 'It's time we got this sorted out. I know you won't be turned out, because the cottage belongs to my aunt, and I also know that she's quite anxious to sell to you, for a very reasonable price.'

Joanna felt indignation rising rapidly as he pulled her across the patio to a far side of the spacious lawn where a tall, distinguished-looking man was talking to the effusive Mrs Stenning-Young.

'Aunt Vera, you've already met Joanna Morris, though I think I should have introduced you to her properly, and this is my father, Joanna, Mrs Stenning-Young's brother.'

'How delightful,' Mrs Stenning-Young gushed. 'Of course, we've already met, and I must repeat how grateful I was for your help with the flower festival, dear. The Bishop tells me that it's all been a great success, brought a lot of new interest to the Cathedral, and we've raised a considerable sum towards the cost of repairing the Cathedral spire. I believe it's you who lives at Willow-Weed. My dear, it's yours, of course. The agent sent your letter on to me and I shall be happy to sell at an agreed price. You'll be hearing from my solicitor, and I've instructed him to take off the amount you paid for the alterations and repairs as well as the three years' rent you've paid. Does that sound fair to you?'

Joanna felt as if the wind had been knocked out of her sails and could only manage a weak smile while she sorted out her thoughts, but the elderly gentleman, so intent on studying a plant growing in a tub, slowly turned, and his smile was such that Joanna felt a rush of warmth surround her.

'My dear—Joanna, if I heard correctly—I'm delighted to meet you.'

Here was a friend, Joanna decided at once as she shook hands with Adam's father. Brother and sister, though? Mr Royston and Mrs Stenning-Young were totally unalike both to look at and in manner.

'I'm pleased to meet you too,' she said. He held her hand longer than was strictly necessary, but she didn't mind, in fact she drew some strength from him—a strength which she felt he saw she needed.

'So you're the young lady living all alone at Willow-Weed Cottage?'

'She doesn't have to any longer,' Adam said. 'Kamla would love to share it with her—and it's only for a year, Joanna.'

Joanna glanced up into Adam's face and something indefinable passed between them, and although she reiterated that she didn't intend to share she knew that he would get his own way eventually.

'Don't be rushed into anything, Joanna. Adam is both impetuous and hasty—give the poor girl time to get used to the idea, Adam,' his father advised as he laid a hand on his son's shoulder, and both men stared down at her until the colour suffused her cheeks.

'I'm sure when you get to know Kamla you'll change your mind,' Mrs Stenning-Young insisted, but Joanna wanted to let the matter drop. She intended to fight to make her own decision even if Adam did prove too strong for her in the end. 'Think how helpful her rent will be in paying all those dreaded monthly bills!'

'I've managed up until now. I've had to learn to be independent——'

'You're that to a fault,' Adam said. 'But I did think you'd welcome female company—you wouldn't be there together that much, I suppose, but it's quite nice to know that there's someone to come home to share some gossip with.'

'I'm never lonely, Adam,' Joanna assured her boss. 'I see people all day so that when I go home I enjoy being able to please myself.'

Adam placed his arm round her waist. 'I can see someone needs a ducking—there are ways *off* making you agree,' he mocked in a bad German accent which made everyone laugh.

'Gentle persuasion, Adam, might bring results. Maybe an unwanted ducking will antagonise a little too much. Are you ready for a swim?' Mr Royston asked.

'Mm—yes, presently perhaps.'

'The lady is too modest,' Adam chanted sarcastically, and guided Joanna along to the edge of the pool where members of the staff were enjoying themselves.

'Would you like a drink before you go in?' he asked. 'White wine? G & T?'

'Just a soft drink, please,' Joanna said, remembering that in order to be ready for Julian it had been necessary to miss a meal, and she was quite hungry.

'Ah, you haven't eaten?' Adam surmised correctly. 'Shouldn't you swim first?'

'An orange squash would be nice,' she said. He went to the table where the drinks were set out and Joanna felt that they were being polite to each other to cover up the underlying tension. He couldn't know how much she dreaded taking off her clothes, even though she was wearing an ample one-piece bathing costume which afforded a neat skirt to cover her thighs. But after a drink, when it seemed Adam had tired of making small talk, he was claimed by the lovely Kamla and Joanna searched desperately for Julian. She needed to talk to him, ask for advice—no, she must stop doing that, she knew exactly what she wanted, the way she intended to live, so there was nothing Julian could say to help her. It was just that he knew her circumstances better than anyone, and at this moment she felt she needed a friend to confide in. She felt a splash of water on her toes and looking down into the side of the pool she saw Julian looking up at her. 'Coming in?' he asked. He grabbed one ankle. 'I could . . .' he teased.

'Please don't,' she said. 'I need to talk to you.'

Julian managed to hide the sigh of impatience as he said: 'Surely not now, Joanna. Nothing can be that urgent. This is a party, so let yourself go, come on in and have some fun. It's getting dusk now, so no one will notice you.' At that moment Lynn popped up beside Julian and promptly ducked his head under water.

'Why are you taking so long, Joanna? Get your dress off and come on in,' she urged.

More of the staff noticed her standing at the side of the pool and it seemed obvious that if she didn't get her clothes off she would find herself in the water fully clothed. Not that she was wearing that much. Over her swimming costume she was wearing a waist slip and a polyester dress in deep pink with white piping at the edge of the short sleeves and down the vee neckline. It was a new outfit with pink bag and sandals to match, so she didn't much fancy having it soaked at its debut.

She took a step back and Lynn pointed to the changing rooms where Joanna found an empty cubicle where she undressed, leaving her belongings in the locker provided, before venturing outside again. She loved to swim and often visited the leisure centre in Tullbury where there was an extra large swimming pool, and she found that by putting all her energy into several lengths the tension of her busy days at Ampfield Hospital diminished. Probably to everyone's surprise she took a dive from the side and swam with strong powerful strokes until she had covered the width and length of the pool. She was instantly acceptable to the rest of the staff, and when she next saw Julian he was having fun with Lynn. She went to the side for a rest and watched, suddenly realising how things were between Julian and Lynn. They looked quite natural together, but then Julian was well liked and popular among the female staff, even though it was assumed that he had a special place in his affections for Joanna. Hadn't she acknowledged the fact that recently they had both become aware of a change in their relationship? It had been a doctor-patient association at first which had grown into a deeper understanding, narrowing into a more intimate relationship when they were living under the same roof and working together, but which had gradually weakened, and now broadened into a happy 'best mate' comfortable friendship.

Was something growing between Lynn and Julian? she wondered. Lynn was her own special friend and they often went to shows and shopping trips together. Lynn and her mother were thoroughly nice people, devoted to each other and warmly welcoming to visitors, especially Joanna, because she had no family close by and lived alone. Did Lynn know of this Indian doctor's appointment? Was she aware—had anyone been aware of Adam's involvement with the foreigner? Her thoughts sped around in her brain until she was forced to admit that it didn't bother her if Julian and Lynn were attracted to each other nearly as much as Adam's relationship with Kamla Ramarsingh! Surely Julian would know about a new appointment, so why hadn't he told her?

'That was an excellent performance, Joanna,' Adam said, breaking into her confusion. He stooped down beside her at the pool's edge. 'Not giving up so soon?'

'Aren't you coming in?' she countered.

'Not just yet, though I believe it's the host's privilege to be thrown in before the end of the party.'

'That doesn't seem quite fair,' Joanna said. 'I should get in first if I were you.'

'I've been eating, so I'll wait awhile. How about you? Aren't you hungry yet?'

'Desperately,' she answered with a smile. 'Swimming always has that effect, doesn't it?'

He held out his hand and she took it eagerly so that he could pull her out of the water.

'You're an excellent swimmer, Joanna, and if I may be personal I like the costume. There's rather more of it than most girls wear these days, but you evidently aim to tantalise the male population.'

'Nothing of the sort,' she snapped. 'I find this style more comfortable.' She left him to run into the changing room where she dried herself and dressed again before going to the patio where sausages were sizzling alongside steaks and burgers of varying sizes. It was a warm, balmy evening with a high moon and brilliant stars. The air was filled with laughter and music, and as Joanna chose what she wanted to eat she was joined by Lynn.

'Having a good time?' her friend asked.

'Yes, it's a nice pool,' Joanna said, 'and a rather splendid house and gardens. I didn't realise it was quite so plush. Somehow I didn't imagine Adam Royston going in for something as ornate and exotic as this.'

Lynn filled her plate and drew Joanna away from the tables. 'Julian has just told me that the house is Kamla's. Her parents have given it to her as a wedding gift.'

'You mean she and Adam——'

'I suppose so. He's obviously mad about her.'

'I've just learned that Willow-Weed belongs to Mrs Stenning-Young who is Adam's aunt, and she's quite willing to sell to me, but——'

'But what?' Lynn questioned eagerly.

'Adam wants me to take Kamla as a—' Joanna shrugged, 'er—paying guest, I suppose. For a year, he said.'

'That'll be nice. Mum keeps on at me to persuade you to get someone to share with you, Joanna.'

'But I don't want to share my home with anyone, Lynn. I've managed on my own for three years and I can go on living that way.'

'I can see your point—you value your independence, but in this case, if Adam and the Indian doctor are to be married then it'll only be for a short time. The money would be useful, wouldn't it, to help with the mortgage and bills?'

'That's what Mrs Stenning-Young suggested, but I've coped up till now with a loan which I've repaid as well as the rent. Buying won't be any more costly and Mrs Stenning-Young has said that she'll take off the alteration bill and the three years' rental from the asking price.'

'Gosh!' Lynn exclaimed after swallowing a large piece of quiche. 'That's considerate of her.'

'Yes, but is it a bribe to get me to agree to take Dr Ramarsingh?'

'Well, they can't force you into anything, but personally I think it's a lovely idea.'

'Trust you—but, think, Lynn. Would you really want to share with a woman you've only just met, and from a different culture from our own? I mean, it could be disastrous—awkward at times if she and Adam are—you know.'

'I believe you're jealous, and there was me thinking how lucky you were to have Julian. If Adam and Kamla want to be cosy they only have to come up here.'

'Why can't she live here in her own home, for goodness' sake?' Joanna asked indignantly.

'Because it just isn't done, apparently, so Julian said.'

'He seems remarkably well informed. She'd be well protected by those ferocious dogs, and that doesn't explain why Adam has to live here.'

'You sound quite bitchy for you, Joanna. There are obviously very good reasons for the way they've arranged things, and you should be flattered that he thinks you're good enough to allow his fiancée to share your home.'

'Can't you see, Lynn? They really wanted Willow-Weed for her, but as it's only for a short time they would be silly to turn down my offer.'

'Joanna!' Lynn said impatiently. 'Stop it! You're getting paranoid about the whole affair. If they really wanted your cottage they only had to give you notice to quit, and when the time comes for Adam and Kamla to get hitched they'd soon make some profit putting Willow-Weed on the market. It's a super cottage if it weren't so isolated.'

'But it's the isolation I need,' Joanna insisted.

'Why? I don't understand you at all. Most girls would jump at the chance of having company. It isn't good for you to be alone so much.'

Joanna withdrew into herself. She had managed to keep her secret for so long by keeping herself to herself and not getting too friendly with anyone but Julian. He knew the truth, he understood her fears and that she didn't want sympathy for the imperfections of her body, and he honoured her request that no one should know, but now wasn't Lynn her best mate? Time, and emotion, were forcing her to make a choice and she desperately needed to talk. She hastily finished her food, then she tapped Lynn's arm as she drew the skirt of her dress aside.

'See this?' she whispered. 'Not a pretty sight, so I don't parade my disfigurement around for all and sundry to see. I suppose you'll tell your mum, I don't mind, but no one else, please, Lynn.'

Lynn looked, and gasped, putting her hand over her mouth to stifle her intake of breath at the sight of the ugly weal on Joanna's upper leg. 'You poor girl! But it's not so drastic, being on your leg, is it?'

'That isn't all, Lynn. The whole of my right side is affected. That's how I met Julian—he was the one who helped me through the bad times. He was my doctor, a very new houseman at the time, but he saw me through the usual skin grafts, and it was partly his influence which led me to take up nursing, and then I came here to specialise in burns and cosmetic surgery—but mainly because he was here to protect me.'

'How did it happen, Joanna? Or—no, don't tell me if it's too painful.'

'Like I said, you and I have been friends for a long time. I couldn't bring myself to actually tell anyone about the accident at first, and when I came here Julian and I thought it best to keep quiet about it.'

'How old were you when the accident happened?'

'Sixteen. As you know, my parents live abroad for most of the time, so Philip, my brother, and I stayed with my mother's two sisters during holidays from boarding school. I'd thought of going on to university to study medicine eventually—paediatrics, probably—but the accident, which happened one Christmas, changed all that. We went to the village hall to a teenage dance. There'd been a fair amount of drinking, although most of the youngsters were local from affluent families and home from school the same as we were. Somehow fire broke out, a cigarette butt carelessly thrown down among papers hats, they thought. Lynn, it's a sight I shall never forget—smoke, flames licking round doors and windows, kids screaming and pushing—it was dreadful.' Joanna paused, remembering.

'Leave the rest until another time,' Lynn said kindly.

'No, I want you to know. Several youngsters were killed, trapped by a locked door at the other end of the hall to where the fire had broken out. I could have pushed my way out through a window with the others, but there was a fourteen-year-old girl there whom I knew. She was illegitimate and had been brought up by her grandparents. I suddenly saw the anguish in their faces if anything should ever happen to Emma and I just knew I had to try to help her. She was a tiny little thing, so she'd got trampled on and was stunned. Carl helped me to drag her towards a side door, but . . . her . . . clothing was well alight and we couldn't get the flames out. It was a nightmare—one that keeps recurring even after nearly nine years.'

'Who's Carl?' Lynn asked, trying to break the memory which was clearly all too vivid in Joanna's mind.

'A friend of my brother's—and—a kind of boyhood sweetheart, I suppose. Our clothing quickly ignited too. I just remember the awful panic and horror before I passed out, and the next thing I knew I was in hospital. It was some time before I realised how badly burnt my side was, and a much longer time before I realised just how it was going to affect my life. What man wants a disfigured woman for a wife?'

'Joanna, you mustn't think like that. It could have been worse, it could have been your face—think of Roxanne.'

'I suppose I must have been crazy to come and work in a place where the very nature of the work keeps the memory of that dreadful night alive. Poor little Emma died, and it broke her grandparents' hearts. And Carl, in trying to help me, and save Emma too, was very badly injured by falling roof timbers, as well as sustaining seventy-five per cent burns.'

'Where is he now, then?' Lynn asked.

Joanna sighed. 'At first we were all taken to Reading Hospital. I stayed in the burns unit for several months while the grafts were done, but Carl was moved to a hospital in London where his parents lived and worked. They have a business of their own, and I think they found a place for Carl there somewhere eventually, but we lost touch.'

'Your parents must have been terribly worried.'

Joanna snorted her disgust. 'They flew home, stayed long enough to see that they didn't have to arrange a funeral and went back to America. My aunts mean much more to me than my parents.'

'What about your brother? Was he burnt too?'

Joanna laughed. 'No, he's the lucky kind, and he'd gone off into the night with the girl he later married. He's five years older than me and was at university studying accountancy. He's Mr Money-Bags now, but he's a dear, and money has never made any difference to him. He and his wife Sheila live in London and they desperately wanted me to go to live with them, but I like to be within visiting distance of my aunts. They're not so young any more and I have a lot to thank them for. We're all quite close, though, and I see Phil and Sheila from time to time. That's why I needed a place of my own, so that they can come to stay in the summer or weekends.' She laughed meaningfully. 'Funny to be a close family yet without our parents. They're the real outsiders.'

'Isn't that rather sad?' Lynn said. 'I think the world of my mum.'

'I know, and I could envy you if I didn't have my two aunts. They spoil me rotten, and my brother would if I let him, but I mean to stand on my own two feet.'

'You can be *too* independent, Joanna.' Lynn got up and went to fetch two glasses of wine. 'Here,' she said gently. 'If anyone needs this it's you, and thanks for telling me. I can understand you much better now—your faith, for one thing, and why you'd never share rooms with another girl. And why you and Julian are so close—but don't get the idea that he's the only man who'd marry you. There are genuine people in the world. True love knows no bounds—the right man will love you, scars and all.'

'I doubt if I shall ever marry anyone,' Joanna said. 'Julian has been good to me and helped me over many a stile, but I can't expect any man to marry such an imperfect specimen as me.'

'That's only your body, Joanna,' Lynn protested. 'Isn't that what you tell your patients? If you don't really believe it then you're being dishonest.'

'We all have to tell little white lies occasionally.'

'It's a pity you've chosen to keep this all to yourself since you came here to Ampfield, Joanna. Once anything is out in the open it gets well aired and then forgotten.'

'But it's not the sort of thing you can tell people—only special friends, and I don't want pity. I have to make the best of my life, and helping others in similar circumstances seems the best way to do it.'

Lynn was quietly thoughtful as they refilled their plates, enjoyed another glass of white wine and then gossiped generally about all that was going on around them. The pool was less crowded now as people dried and dressed, and soft romantic melodies wafted in the evening air, inviting couples to dance. The patio was large with clean white paving slabs expertly laid, and a pergola, fragrant with the scent of summer roses and honeysuckle, made the ideal place for surreptitious kisses to be exchanged between members of the staff. Joanna noticed that Adam had escorted his father and aunt to their car and then returned to take Kamla into his arms. Her sari, made of Indian silk, swayed gently as they danced, her small, even white teeth sparkling as she laughed up at him in the subdued lighting, which came from fancy coloured bulbs strung out like a brilliant necklace along the edge of the patio from tree to tree, and all through the pergola. As darkness shrouded the garden a magic enchantment settled among the partygoers, and Joanna quickly forgot all about the cottage and the conversation she'd had with Lynn. Julian remained in the pool, swimming until he was the sole occupant, then he went to change before coming to claim Joanna as his partner, but they had hardly had time to exchange a brief word when Adam tapped Julian on the shoulder.

'An unofficial excuse-me,' he said lightheartedly, and Joanna, while thrilled to be in his arms, dreaded the inquisition she expected. But he hardly spoke, just held her tightly so that the warmth of his hands through the light material of her dress made her body tingle with satisfaction. The satisfaction of knowing that he was enjoying holding her—but he didn't know what hideous scars her dress was hiding, and was this loving feeling just to make her reconsider her refusal to have Kamla stay at Willow-Weed? She was glad that Adam was holding her against his massive chest, and his being so tall meant that her face was well below his so that he couldn't see the stray tear which trickled obstinately down her cheek. If this was just a one-off incident then she must make the most of it.

She felt the rumble in his throat against her head as he hummed lightly to the tune of the love song which was altogether too smoochy, and then without warning the tempo changed to *Viva Espana*. The mood of the party became less subdued and more uninhibited, and without warning Joanna found herself being jostled along towards the pool where Adam was destined to be thrown. It was useless to plead, and Adam deliberately kept hold of her, so that with a great splash they found themselves floundering in the water. Joanna's dress seemed as if it must be waterproof at first as it spread out around her, but she managed to pull the skirt down at the sides while eager hands urged her towards the side, where she was hauled out. Someone produced towelling robes, one for herself and one for Adam. 'An initiation, I suppose you could say,' he said with a broad grin all across his face. 'Sorry about the dress, but most materials are washable these days.'

Joanna dried her face, then began to feel angry at what might have happened to her new bag and sandals. It was Kamla who placed an arm round her and drew her into the house. 'Up into the bathroom, Joanna,' she said firmly. 'I have a spare sari which will do for you to wear home. Have a warm shower and I'll put clean underwear out for you.'

Joanna took off the wet clothes and put them in the bath before she stepped into a luxuriously designed shower cubicle. She felt a sense of urgency and almost wished that it had been Lynn who had come to her rescue, but this, of course, was Kamla's house. Thank goodness her brunette hair was natural and the ducking only added to its waviness, so she allowed the warm water to completely wash over her so that she began to glow with warmth. Then it occurred to her that Adam might be waiting to use the shower, so she turned off the water and opened the glass panelled door. To her surprise a bath sheet had been placed over the nearby towel rail, and clean undies on a chair, so she dried herself quickly and put them on, but they didn't cover her scars. What was she to do? She had only just met Kamla Ramarsingh, even if she was a qualified doctor. If Kamla saw her disfigurement she would be certain to tell Adam, and that she couldn't bear. In any case, she could hardly emerge from the bathroom wearing such scant briefs and bra. Suddenly there was a knock at the bathroom door.

'Joanna? Are you all right?' To her horror it was Adam's voice. She looked around for her own wet clothes, but someone had been in and removed them.

'Yes, of course,' she answered in a husky voice, 'but I can hardly go home like this.'

She heard him chuckle. 'Don't panic,' he said smugly. 'Kamla has a sari here, but I expect you'll need help putting it on. Come along to her bedroom so that I can use the shower.' She heard the knob turn and he swept in. Joanna grabbed the towel to cover herself with, but Adam seemed bent only on removing the towel around his lower half and stepping into the shower cubicle. She felt her cheeks taut with confusion, but she was eager to get away and hurried out of the bathroom and into the next room where Kamla was waiting.

'Adam was quite prepared for such an event, but not you, I think, my dear,' Kamla laughed. 'Don't worry, we'll recompense you for any damage done to your clothes—now, take that damp towel away, and . . .' A tug-of-war ensued for the towel, and when Joanna was forced to give in a stifled silence kept them apart as Kamla surveyed the pattern of cobbled skin which snaked from Joanna's shoulder to her upper thigh. The moment passed, and without a word Kamla draped the sari over Joanna's shoulder and proceeded to instruct her how to wear it.

CHAPTER FIVE

JOANNA felt that she should be protesting. Wasn't it something of an imposition to be wearing the dress of another country?

'Joanna,' Kamla said softly, 'you look quite beautiful.'

Joanna stiffened. Was she being patronising? Was there a hint of pity? 'Hardly that,' she said. 'And I do feel a fraud wearing something which clearly belongs to India.'

'We couldn't let you go home in wet things, my dear, and the party isn't over yet. A nice hot cup of coffee now to warm you up, after you've dried your hair.' Kamla secured the sari at Joanna's waist and pushed the hairdryer into her hand. Joanna stood before a full-length mirror as she fanned her hair dry, running her fingers through it to aid the process. Her cheeks were quite flushed with embarrassment as she met Kamla's gaze in their reflections, and in a few moments she switched off the appliance and handed it back to Kamla.

'Thank you,' she said, 'but I usually let it dry naturally.'

'How lucky you are to have such natural hair, Joanna. You have a good figure too, just right for wearing a sari, though in India we say that a sari is good for the fuller figure. It hides those middle-age unwanted bulges. I'd like you to keep it, that's if you aren't offended.'

'I couldn't, Kamla,' Joanna said quickly, 'I agree it's lovely, and it feels so soft and graceful to wear, but . . .'

'Then it's yours. You may need something to wear for a fancy dress party, perhaps? Or even an evening gown at the hospital ball?'

Joanna shook her hair free before styling it with her comb which she found lying on the bed along with other belongings out of her bag.

'I'm sorry everything got so wet,' Kamla apologised.

'I expect the bag and sandals will dry out, and my dress

64

will wash.'

'It was a special outfit, I think,' Kamla observed. 'Quite new?'

'Yes,' Joanna admitted. 'My aunt made the dress for me, she's a very talented needlewoman, so I bought bag and sandals to match, but they weren't expensive ones.'

'We'll dry them out, of course, and meanwhile here is a small bag for your personal things, and a pair of sandals. I think we take the same size.'

'This really isn't necessary, Kamla. I'm sure Julian would have taken me straight home even dripping wet. I must admit that it was a surprise to find myself being thrown in like that.'

Kamla laughed. 'You're a good sport, Joanna. We have to be, though, working in a hospital, don't we?'

'What made you come to Ampfield of all places?' Joanna dared to ask.

'Because I want to study burns treatments and cosmetic surgery, and what better countryside to be in than here overlooking the Wiltshire plains?' Kamla paused and looked directly into Joanna's eyes. 'I understand now why you came to Ampfield, and I think it was a very brave thing to do. May I ask about your accident, or is that too presumptuous of me?'

Joanna looked away. Once tonight was enough, surely, she told herself, but if she didn't explain the situation to Kamla, by morning all the hospital might know. Hesitantly she told the story again, but only with the briefest of details, adding: 'Before this evening no one except Julian knew, and that's the way I prefer it to be. No one else must ever know, not even Adam.'

'But being in charge here, don't you think——?'

'No!' Joanna was positive. 'Please, can you forget what you saw? I'm grateful for your kindness this evening, this sari is lovely for covering everything up, but now you understand why I prefer to live alone, and why I value my independence.'

Kamla smiled with genuine warmth. 'Of course,' she said. 'Let's go and find that coffee.'

As they went down the wide curving staircase members of the staff who had drifted into the spacious hall looked up, and as they saw Joanna beside Kamla gasps of admiration escaped their lips. Julian pushed his way to the bottom of the stairs. 'Are you all right, Joey?' he asked with whispered concern.

'Yes, of course,' she replied with a smile. 'I've always admired Indian women being able to wear such graceful clothes, but I never expected to find myself in a sari. It was worth being thrown in the pool.'

'Quite the belle of the ball,' a voice said behind her, and at the foot of the stairs Adam put his arm round her. 'A sari suits you, Joanna, and I hope I'm forgiven for taking you in the pool with me? I suppose it was rather thoughtless, but I'll gladly reimburse you for any damage done to your clothes.'

'It was an exclusive dress made by Joanna's aunt,' Kamla interrupted. 'But we wouldn't expect a mere man to understand such things, would we, Joanna?' Her dark eyes were filled with mischief. 'It's going to cost you, Adam.'

'No, really, I'm sure it'll wash all right. By the way, where is it?'

'We'll get it laundered for you, Joanna, it's the least we can do,' Kamla said. 'Now come with me.' She led the way into the dining room which was laid out with tables of food, wine and other beverages. Joanna noticed that many of the guests had left and the people remaining had come into either the dining room or lounge, which were linked by glass doors now standing open as well as the sliding patio doors in both rooms opening out on to the garden. Several of her colleagues admired the sari as she fetched her coffee, and when she turned to look for Julian she noticed him in earnest conversation with Adam. Lynn pulled Joanna back outside into the deserted hall. 'Did you mind?' she asked.

'About being thrown into the pool? With Adam? You must be joking,' she said happily. 'It was rather embarrassing having to borrow underwear and to have Kamla dress me, so——' she paused and raised her eyebrows at Lynn. 'She knows all there is to know about me now.'

'Well, maybe that's not such a bad idea if she's going to share your cottage.'

'Hang on,' Joanna said. 'Who says she is? No way. I'm thrilled about being able to buy Willow-Weed and I'm staying there alone, so it's no use anyone trying to persuade me otherwise.' A strange tingle ran up her spine, but she really meant what she said. No one, but no one was going to change her mind!

The girls mingled, Joanna putting on an air of careless abandon, and later when she looked around for Julian intending to suggest that they went home there was no sign of him or Lynn. Adam came to her rescue.

'Looking for Julian? He's taken Lynn home and I said I'd take you,' he stated flatly.

'But . . . Julian brought us together,' she said.

'A threesome? Come on now, that's hardly cricket. Lynn didn't seem to mind, so I hope you don't either?'

She dared to glance up into his chocolate-coloured eyes. His expression was one of self-satisfaction at his scheming and she realised that he had noticed something she hadn't. 'You are rather sweetly naïve, my dear Joanna,' he said. 'Don't you realise that Julian has been using you to get to Lynn?'

'You're quite wrong,' she said hurriedly, then realised that without giving some details about her past she couldn't clarify that positive statement. 'Well,' she added, 'I don't think Julian needed to use me to get to Lynn. We're all unattached and he's quite capable of pursuing anyone he fancies.'

She didn't like the way Adam grinned and gently rubbed his fingers up her arm. 'A sari suits you very well,' he said. 'Perhaps makes you appear a trifle slimmer, and heaven knows you're slim enough. I hope you'll wear it to all the hospital dances.'

'I couldn't,' she said. 'It wouldn't seem right.'

'For goodness' sake stop being so modest, Joanna. I presume you're ready to go home?'

'Yes, I am. I'm on duty at nine o'clock tomorrow morning.'

'Then we'd better get going.'

Joanna went to find Kamla to thank her for her hospitality and the loan of the clothes and then she found herself sitting beside Adam in his low sports car. He had the roof down, and as they sped through the country lanes the wind blew her hair around her face and fanned her body through the fine silk of the sari.

'Why didn't you tell me before that it was your aunt who

owned Willow-Weed?' Joanna asked as they drew up in front of the cottage.

'It didn't seem important, Joanna,' he replied stiffly. 'Not until we realised that Kamla would have to find somewhere to live for the time being. Portia House is much too large for her to live in alone, and in this day and age we can't leave it unoccupied, which is why I've taken up residence there, while Kamla has been in London working.' He pulled himself out of the car and was round to help Joanna out before she had time to unfold her legs from the tangle of soft silk gathered round her ankles. There was a strained silence as she put the key into the lock and opened the solid oak door.

'Thank you very much for bringing me home,' she said, turning to face him. 'It was a good party.'

He smiled suddenly, bringing crinkles of amusement to the corners of his large dark eyes. 'Even getting a soaking?'

'It could have been worse,' she said, 'but Kamla was very kind. I hadn't heard that we were to have a new doctor at Ampfield.'

'I'm sure you'll find her easy to work with—and dare I say that I'm hoping you'll change your mind about having her stay with you?'

'I'm sorry, Adam, it wouldn't work,' she said firmly. 'If the sale of the cottage goes through without any hitches, which your aunt seems to think it will, then I prefer to carry on alone.'

'But her contract with Ampfield is only for a year, then she may well move on somewhere else or return to her family in India.'

'I heard she was planning to marry.'

Adam raised his eyebrows. 'News travels fast,' he said. 'Nothing definite is planned, certainly not during the year she's studying here.' A frown creased his brow as if he had been reminded of something unpleasant, but Joanna couldn't imagine what she might have said out of place. She led the way through into her lounge where a light had been left on, and by the way Adam hovered she assumed he was expecting to be offered some refreshment, but it was after midnight and she was anxious to get to bed. She wouldn't sleep, of course. So much was on her mind. The very fact that Willow-Weed was to be hers, and acquired so easily, was enough excitement to keep her wide awake for several hours yet, but that excitement was overshadowed somewhat by the need to tell Lynn and Kamla about her accident. She didn't want to dwell on that, and she hoped they would honour her request to keep it to themselves. Lynn would, she knew, but could she vouch for Kamla's discretion? As a doctor she should be able to keep a confidence, but it depended how involved she was with Adam. Then there was Lynn and Julian to think about. It had come as a shock to Joanna to learn that they were attracted to one another. She supposed she was too close to both of them to have noticed, but in a way she was pleased, because she didn't want Julian to think of her as anything more than a friend. He'd always be that, she thought, a very dear genuine friend, and what could be nicer than he and Lynn becoming more than just working colleagues?

'Well?' Adam broke into her reverie. 'Don't I get a drink for bringing you home?'

Joanna looked at him without really seeing him for a moment, then she very nearly retorted that she hadn't asked him to bring her home, but the softness in his expression made her respond as she would normally do to a guest. Somewhere deep inside her heart was an ache which was getting stronger by the minute. Was it due to the arrival of Kamla Ramarsingh? Could it be jealousy? She guessed it must be to cause her to feel so contrary, and she felt angry with herself for allowing it to happen.

'Of course,' she said brightly. 'What would you like? Tea, coffee, cocoa, or sherry, which I'm afraid is all I have in the house.'

'A good old-fashioned cup of cocoa sounds just what we both need after so much indulgence.' He joined her in the kitchen while Joanna warmed the milk and put cocoa in mugs set on a tray. Outside an owl hooted and kept calling its mate, which drew Joanna to the window.

'He often comes after dark,' she said. 'I never thought I'd get used to the strange noises of country life after living in the town.'

Suddenly Adam grabbed her by her arms and pulled her up against him. 'Who are you trying to convince that you feel safe and secure here on your own?'

'But I do, Adam,' she said adamantly. 'Three years is quite enough time to know what I want, and *you've* never been concerned before.'

'Because I thought you and Julian were probably going to get married at any time. I presumed that he took good care of you.'

'And he has done ever since I came to Ampfield.'

'But things have been changing, haven't they? I'm observant enough to notice that there isn't quite the twinkle in his eyes when your name is mentioned that there was at the beginning.'

'So?' she questioned haughtily. 'We were very close, we still are, but in a different way.'

'So you're admitting that your relationship has cooled considerably?'

Joanna shrugged as she picked up the tray and walked round him to lead the way into the lounge. She had been expecting an inquisition, but not about her relationship with Julian.

'There's nothing to admit,' she retorted. 'I know that you take an interest in all the staff at Ampfield, but what there is or has been between Julian and myself is really none of your business.'

He came close towards her again as she straightened up from putting the tray down on the low glass-topped table, and before she could protest he was holding her much too closely. She could smell the tangy fragrance of his aftershave and remembered how he had barged in on her in the bathroom at Portia House. Funny feelings were dancing around her beneath the sari and the delicate material shimmering next to her skin made her feel less than confident. If only Julian had brought her home! That she could have coped with, but Adam's sudden interest was almost too much to bear, especially as she had only just recently begun to realise her own feelings for him.

'You can't shut yourself away from everyone by living here alone,' Adam said gruffly. 'Julian and Lynn must be given space to work out their relationship, and you must get on with the business of living.'

'Look!' Joanna said indignantly, pulling away from him forcefully. 'I've never interfered in any way between Julian and anyone else. I don't own him, nor he me. We're very good friends and likely to remain that way, I hope. If he and Lynn are ——'

'It leaves you out on a limb,' Adam cut in. 'And that concerns me, Joanna. Julian will be otherwise occupied and not able to keep an eye on you here at Willow-Weed. In spite of your apparent indifference I believe you're going to miss him.'

'Well—yes, of course I shall miss his company, but there are other fish in the sea, and *I* shall be free to do my own thing without any interference from anyone.'

Adam took a step back from her as if scalded, a frown darkened his expression, so she handed him his mug of cocoa and willed him to leave. But he wasn't so easily fobbed off. He sat down in the nearest easy chair, one which was large and comfortable, so that he looked at home with his long legs sprawled out across the carpet. Joanna's heart sang at the homely sight, but every now and then it skipped a beat as she anticipated the topic of conversation she knew he intended to re-open.

'I can assure you,' he said at length, 'Kamla is a delightful person—clean-living, happy, dedicated to her work and good company.'

'And she has a magnificent home. Why would anyone with a house like Portia House need to come and live in a small cottage like this?'

'Because,' he said slowly, and then after deep contemplation drank his cocoa and stood up. 'I can see you're determined to remain as stubborn as women usually are, so for the moment we'll let it rest—and that is what I suggest you get for what's left of the night.'

He strode out of the front door without saying goodnight, and Joanna felt sick inside. Stubborn? How dared he say she was being stubborn as if it were some kind of disease! It was her cottage and whether she shared or not had to be her decision. She flapped around the cottage doing nothing in particular, and finally went to bed and fumed until sleep from exhaustion shielded her from her worries.

Rain fell in great torrents as Joanna drove into Ampfield next morning. It was unbelievable after the warm, sunny day yesterday. She held a nylon mac over her head and shoulders to run into the entrance after parking her beetle and was met by Dennis, the porter, who was just leaving.

'Morning, Joanna,' he said bluntly. 'Thought you had enough of a ducking last night without wishing this on me on my day off.'

'If it's your day off what are you doing here?' she returned equally bluntly.

'Ugh! Sounds like the morning after the night before. Trust me to have to work while everyone else was having fun. I was on duty from midnight until eight. I've just had my breakfast and now I suppose I can go home to sleep. Nothing else you can do on a day like today.'

'It could be a summer storm, Dennis,' Joanna said patiently. 'By the time you've had a good sleep the sun will be shining. What had you planned to do anyway?'

He grinned sheepishly. 'I was going to ask you to go to the beach with me,' he said. 'Didn't know you was such a good swimmer.'

Joanna laughed. 'It was just as well I could swim, wasn't it? Thanks for the invitation to the beach, Dennis, some other time maybe, but I reckon I shall go home and be lazy when I go off duty this afternoon.'

The sound of an ambulance siren broke through the barrier of falling rain, and Dennis made a bolt for his car before he got caught for extra duty. Joanna smiled to herself as she went upstairs in the lift. Dear Dennis, the kind of twenty-year-old any girl would like to have for a brother—and thinking of brothers, she must remember to telephone Philip later today. He'd be chuffed about Willow-Weed as he loved the country and enjoyed staying with her for the occasional weekend, though they had to be diplomatic so as not to upset the elderly aunts who insisted on Philip and his family staying there when they came down from London.

Up on the nurses' station Joanna listened carefully to a full report of all the patients in her care, and when her colleague had left Joanna started on a tour of the wards. She started at the top in the Intensive Care Unit where Night Sister was handing over to Audrey.

'Still not that much change in Mr King's condition, but if anything slightly more hopeful. He responds to young Matthew, if you can call opening his eyes responding, so if Matthew is happy to sit beside his father then it seems a good idea,' Sister was saying.

'Matthew certainly seems keen,' Joanna said. 'He chatters away about his father now, and he's taking an interest in all that Miss Bennett gives him to do as well. His breathing is very much improved, so let's hope that his father suddenly wakes up to all that's going on around him.'

'I did think that Mrs King seemed irritated by the fact that Matthew was spending time up here with his dad,' Audrey said thoughtfully. 'I can't help wondering if she's blaming Matthew for her husband's condition and Matthew has sensed it.'

'I've questioned that his being so withdrawn was entirely due to the fire,' Joanna said. 'A word with Dr O'Brien might be useful, don't you think, Sister?'

Kathy Murphy was a devotee of the old school of nursing ethics. She was sharp-tongued, brisk and precise, and grumbled constantly about the more familiar attitudes among staff regardless of status, and between staff and patient, but for all that she was one of the most warm-hearted women at Ampfield. She didn't set too much store by psychiatrists, but Dr O'Brien, being a fellow Irishman, could do no wrong.

'Yes indeed, Sister Morris, it would,' she agreed. 'While the little boy has cheered up since visiting his father he appears to have some burden weighing him down, and it isn't right in one so young. Is Dr O'Brien due to come into Ampfield in the near future?'

'Well, if he isn't I can always get in touch with him. I'd better check it out with Dr Royston or Dr West first.'

'Yes, of course. I'll leave it with you. Until Mr King begins to talk we can't judge the situation, but there are often underlying niggles which come to light later,' Sister said. She looked through the window at the patients and pointed out the name Malvin in the report. 'I'm glad to see the Malvin parents are showing signs of recovery, but Elizabeth is still in need of special attention. The two little ones seem to be well on the road to recovery, so as soon as Mr and Mrs Malvin can leave intensive care they can share one of the new units.'

Kathy Murphy finished her report and then hurried away to go to Mass, leaving Joanna to visit her patients alone. She returned to the children's ward where Matthew greeted her with a warm hug as well as several others who were not confined to bed when she heard voices behind her. She turned and for a moment did not recognise the woman accompanying Adam, but when Kamla smiled Joanna knew but was surprised at the change. She appreciated now what Kamla had said about a sari hiding the bulges. In a dark red dress beneath the white coat she looked more than just plump. She was tall and well built but with slim shapeless legs, and Joanna wondered what Adam could possibly see in her. Then Joanna felt guilty—such thoughts were jealous ones, and didn't she know just how kind Kamla was, with a delightful personality? Looks and size were unimportant, just as her own scars were. They didn't influence one's character—or shouldn't, she reprimanded herself.

'Good morning, Joanna,' Adam said, and in reply she nodded to both of her visitors. 'Kamla couldn't wait until tomorrow to start and as Sunday is usually quite a quiet day it's not such a bad idea. So we're doing a quick round and then Kamla is going to do a tracheostomy on a new case admitted this morning. The patient is deteriorating rather rapidly, so it will be a transfer then to Intensive Care. I think Kamla should only remain throughout the morning, so I shall return to pick her up at one o'clock.' He turned to Kamla and smiled. 'Joanna will give you any help you need and when the tracheostomy is done I suggest you meet her in the canteen for coffee, then she can show you over her floor in more detail. From tomorrow you'll be under Julian's wing when I'm not around.'

Kamla glanced down at Matthew and David, who were

standing beside Joanna looking in awe at the new face.

'It looks as if you are well protected, Joanna,' Kamla laughed. 'They are suspicious of me.'

'This is Dr Ramarsingh,' Joanna explained hurriedly. 'You'll be seeing a lot of her from now on as she has come to help Dr Royston and Dr West.'

'My dad's in intensive care,' Matthew said with importance. 'I'm trying to help him wake up.'

At once Kamla bent down and held Matthew by the hand. 'I'm sure he hears you when you speak to him, Matthew,' she said gently. 'He justs needs a rather long rest, but you keep up your vigil.'

'What's vigil mean?' David interrupted.

'Watching and waiting—to keep alert to any sign of change,' Kamla explained. 'I shall be keeping vigil too, in the hope that your father will soon speak to me.'

'You don't know my father,' Matthew accused rather rudely.

'I have just been to see him. I'm looking forward to getting to know everyone here at the hospital.' Kamla stood up straight and glanced at Adam knowingly; then Joanna sent the boys off while she told Kamla all about the children in the ward.

The Indian doctor had a lovely way with the children and Joanna felt she was going to be an asset in many respects. It was some time since a female doctor had been assigned to Ampfield. The last one, Joanna remembered, had left about fifteen months ago when it had become obvious that she was paying too much attention to the male staff and Adam in particular. Adam had gained his reputation then of being a woman-hater, certainly he disliked women doctors and had vowed that he would never accept another one at Ampfield. He had declared that the female nursing staff were enough to manage as it was. Yet the more you got to know him the nicer he seemed to be, Joanna decided. The term 'Godfather' was appropriate. He admitted that he had taken it for granted that Julian looked after her, so until now he had appeared not to be interested in her affairs. But was the sudden change because he had been astute enough to notice that Julian and Lynn were

becoming better acquainted, or was it because of Kamla's
appointment here? And had he arranged it all? she wondered.
Willow-Weed was the answer of course! But what she couldn't
fathom was why, if Kamla had spent last night at Portia House
with Adam, she couldn't continue to live in her own house.
One thing was certain—that no matter how nice Kamla was
Joanna was remaining at her cottage alone. Joanna followed
them through the wards on her floor listening to Adam give a
brief résumé about each patient, and when they reached the
door Adam said: 'I'll give you a ring when Kamla's ready to go
for coffee, Joanna, you can show her the ropes.' He smiled
stiffly and she remembered how he had left her cottage the
previous evening, or rather early this morning. He was still
feeling sour with her, she supposed, and by bringing Kamla
into Ampfield today, and suggesting that Joanna take her to
the canteen, he hoped Kamla would be able to change her
mind. No way, she thought as she watched them disappear
towards the lift. Kamla was his responsibility and he must find
her somewhere else to live. Perhaps she was resident in the
doctor's quarters, so why bother to move?

Sunday was usually a fairly quiet day in the wards when
preparations for afternoon visitors took priority, but there were
some dressings to be changed and in the case of severe burns
an analgesic tablet was given to lessen the pain. With sterile
mask, gown and gloves Joanna and her staff nurse carried out
this procedure with great care for the young patients who had
gradually come to trust Joanna and her team.

She was beginning to feel in need of refreshment by the time
she had finished, but she had to wait a further half-hour before
a phone call requested that she meet Dr Ramarsingh in
Outpatients. She pulled down her sleeves and tidied herself,
then reported off duty for twenty minutes.

As she stepped out of the lift she was met by Adam, but
there was no sign of Kamla. He supported her by her elbow
and drew her into a quiet corner of the waiting area where they
were hidden by an abundance of tall plants and flowers.

'I'm counting on you to give all the assistance you can to
Kamla,' he said.

'Of course, Adam,' she replied indignantly. 'But I'm sure

all the staff will.'

He gazed down at Joanna with a degree of contempt. She sensed some inexplicable conflict and braced herself for a continuation of his impatience with her for her so-called stubbornness.

'Kamla is very capable,' he went on. 'Work will be no problem, and about the other matter—I do appreciate that if you buy Willow-Weed you'll want to live there by yourself. I can see that entertaining boyfriends could pose a problem. As you so rightly say, one's freedom is to be valued, so don't give the matter another thought. I'm sorry if you felt that I was interfering in your private life, but I'm pleased for you that you're in a position to buy the cottage.' He thrust his hands into his trouser pockets and drew himself up as if to make such an apology cost him dearly. Joanna didn't know what to say. She felt as if she had received a very short, sharp smack!

CHAPTER SIX

KAMLA came through from the downstairs treatment room.
She had discarded her white coat and Joanna felt that the dark
red dress did little for her figure, but the inner glow which
radiated from her expression confirmed that everything Adam
had said about her was true.

'Have I kept you waiting?' Kamla said, touching Joanna's
arm lightly. 'The tracheostomy took a little longer than I'd
thought, and the patient was very distressed.'

'What kind of accident was it?' Joanna asked, moving
towards the lift.

'An electrical toaster which didn't pop up as it should have
done. It was left unattended by the young man who lives in a
flat alone and the next thing he knew the curtains were ablaze.
He had the window open too, which didn't help, and on top of
that he tried to put the fire out himself. In minutes the flat was
filled with smoke, so I'm afraid he has inhaled a considerable
amount. We've put him on a ventilator and he's being
carefully monitored, but I'd like to get back to him as soon as
possible.'

'I'm not off until two o'clock,' Joanna said, 'and I'm hungry,
so I hope you won't mind if I have something to eat?'

'Not at all. I envy you slim people being able to eat just
when you like. After Adam's party last night I must be very
firm with myself. As you can see, weight is a constant battle, it
sometimes is as we get older.'

'But you're not old, Kamla.'

The Indian doctor laughed. 'The wrong side of thirty, I'm
afraid, and heading for forty, but what does age matter? It's
what we do with our lives that counts, and for me my
profession is the most important.'

'Adam says that you're here for a year, and then—marriage?'

'Don't believe all the rumours you hear, but even if I do

marry I want to continue with my work.'

They had reached the counter in the cafeteria and Joanna ordered two coffees and a roll, butter and cheese for herself.

'I think I must look the other way,' Kamla said. 'We are to have lunch with Adam's aunt and his father today, so I must work up a good appetite, which won't be difficult where Mrs Stenning-Young's cooking is concerned.'

Joanna realised that Kamla knew Adam and his family very well indeed and she felt at a disadvantage, but she enjoyed sharing the quarter of an hour with the newcomer and they were soon chatting like old friends. When it was time to return on duty Joanna led the way down the stairs, explaining to Kamla what was situated on each of the floors until they reached the ground floor again.

'You'll soon find your way about,' Joanna told her. 'I expect you'll be visiting my floor quite often.'

'I'm sure I shall, I hope you'll understand that right now I'd like to get back to my young man. Before we go our separate ways, though, Joanna, there is something I must say. I think Adam quite ruthlessly took you for granted—your kind nature—and that is an unforgivable thing to do. I'd like nothing better than to share your home with you; as Adam has told me, you are a special person. You must know from your training days that sharing with someone you don't like or can't trust can make life miserable, but he should have been much more diplomatic in his approach. I hope there won't be any bad feeling between us about it. I do really understand and I'll visit the agents in Tullbury to see what accommodation is available. And,' Kamla added with slightly raised eyebrows, 'I hope you won't hold it against Adam. He was thinking of me and doing what he thought was best, but I'm sure we'll work something out.'

Joanna hesitated, then on an impulse she said: 'Kamla, it isn't that I don't want you to come to Willow-Weed, but the suggestion did come out of the blue. Can I have a bit more time to think about it? After all, you haven't seen where I live and it might not suit you. Perhaps we can arrange some off-duty at the same time so that you can visit me, then we'll take it from there.'

Kamla stood directly in front of Joanna, placing both hands on Joanna's arms. 'I'd like that,' she said. 'I hope we can make it soon. Everyone needs a friend in a strange place and it will take a week or two to get acquainted with the staff here, even though they've made me very welcome so far. Please don't think you must agree to Adam's suggestion, though, just because we are friends. Be very sure you feel happy about the arrangement. There's nothing worse than being pressurised into something against your will.'

'I promise I'll be totally honest,' Joanna said. 'Though already you know more about me than most of the staff here,' she added in a whisper.

'I shall look forward to visiting you soon, Joanna,' Kamla said, and Joanna turned away, wondering what had come over her to change her mind. No, I haven't changed my mind, she told herself. Asking someone to visit was just a friendly gesture and she could still stick to her guns. Willow-Weed was hers, or going to be, and she could please herself. She couldn't explain why she felt this underlying urge to comply with Adam's request, though. Deep down she despised him for suggesting that she might want to entertain boyfriends on the quiet—and why shouldn't she? she demanded fiercely. Julian was the only likely person she would be entertaining, but of course, Adam wasn't to know that. She guessed that Adam had only said what he had to goad her into changing her mind. Was she going to let him succeed?

For the remainder of the morning her private thoughts revolved around the proposed invitation to Kamla. She could visualise the Indian woman making herself at home at Willow-Weed and the picture was not an unattractive one, but still her stubbornness persisted. She would not give in too readily and give Adam the satisfaction of getting his own way. Framed in her mind's eye was a constant miniature of his features. That enigmatic smile, the dark sometimes wicked sparkle in his eyes, and always the brisk manner with which he approached his work. Up until recently she had admired him from afar, known that there was a stronger feeling towards him than she felt for other doctors she worked with, but because there had been Julian she had not allowed her feelings to develop. She supposed she was flattered by his interest in her of late, even though she knew it was only for Kamla's benefit. If she let Kamla move in with her he would be a frequent visitor, but she wasn't sure that she could endure the pain of seeing them together at such close quarters.

Lunches were finished and Joanna was checking that everything was in order before she went off duty when Julian casually walked through the swing doors of the children's ward. He took his time reaching her beside Susie Malvin's cot.

'Hi, Joey,' he said in a low voice.

'Oh dear,' Joanna replied gently. 'Feeling tired after last evening?'

'Mm, though I shouldn't, as I've only just come on duty. The new doctor has just dealt with the bad case in this morning, so for a moment I'm not needed, it seems. Thought I'd just check on my favourite Sister.'

'Oh yes?' Joanna retorted snidely. 'Shouldn't you be checking on your patients?'

'Since it's Sunday, with visitors to prepare for, you nurses prefer us doctors to keep out of your hair, I've noticed.'

'It is a bit hectic on Sundays and we like to give our patients top priority, especially the ones who only get visitors at the weekends. I know people can come in any afternoon, but so many of our cases are brought in from some distance away, so it can make things awkward for some of the patients. They do need to see relatives and friends. What would I have done without my aunts?'

'You had me,' Julian said quickly.

'And I shall be eternally grateful, Julian. By the way, I've actually told Lynn about my accident and how you and I met. And Kamla.'

Julian raised his eyebrows. 'Now that I consider is a good step in the right direction, Joey.'

'I didn't have much choice where Kamla was concerned. Being thrown in the pool did put me in a spot, especially as Adam was in a hurry to get in the shower after me, and Kamla was so anxious to dress me up in that sari, she could hardly not notice my scars.'

'I thought you looked stunning, and so did everyone else.

Kamla seems a very charming woman.'

'Did you know she was coming to Ampfield?'

'Adam mentioned that a friend of his had been appointed here for a year, but I didn't take that much notice. He refrained from saying that it was a "she" and Indian.'

'It all seems to be something of a mystery, don't you think?'

'Not you as well? The grapevine is in danger of being torn down with speculation about Adam and Kamla. I knew that Portia House belonged to a friend of his and that he was sort of house-sitting for the time being, but rumour has it that it's a wedding gift to Kamla in readiness for her marriage, but I'm not sure it's to Adam. If it were I think he would have introduced her to us as his future wife.'

'He's not the kind of man who would want us all to know of his personal plans, though, Julian. He's certainly very fond of her, anyone could see that.'

'So? I'm very fond of you, enough to have embarked on marriage if you'd wanted it.'

'Julian! People don't *embark* on marriage! Doesn't it have to be by mutual consent with some measure of love involved?' Joanna faced him squarely and turned away as quickly to walk out of the children's ward and to her desk, with Julian following slowly.

'I thought we had a fair sized measure of love between us—but you've changed.'

'Are you sure it isn't you who has changed—or both of us perhaps? What about you and Lynn?' Joanna questioned with an affectionate smile.

Julian's boyish features clouded darkly with annoyance. 'What about me and Lynn? Just because Adam asked me to take her home you think we're shacking up together?'

'I know Lynn better than that. She has her mother to consider, and knowing her as I do she'll always consider her come what may, even though I know Mrs Dalton is very keen to see Lynn married off to some real nice guy—and that could so easily be you—Mr Nice Guy,' she added, leaning towards him provocatively.

'What is this?' Julian asked. 'Are you trying to tell me something? Are you trying to fob me off on to Lynn because you've found someone else?'

Joanna tut-tutted in mock disgust. 'Who'd be interested in me, for heavens's sake? Of course there's no one else, Julian.'

'But you're very attractive and everyone goes a bundle on you, Joey.'

'Umph! Until they see the scars, and then they'd run a mile.'

'Don't underestimate people. Beauty is only skin deep anyway, and I think Adam has begun to take a real shine to you.'

'Now you are imagining things. Surely you can see that it's only because he wants Kamla to live in my cottage. As it's only for a year I may decide to agree—what do you think?'

'It might cramp my style a bit,' Julian replied cheekily, giving her ear a tweak. 'Seriously, though, I think it's a super idea. I'm glad too that you can buy Willow-Weed, you'll have security, and if you need any help with seeing the solicitor and mortgage people you know I'll do anything I can, though since it's Adam's aunt who's selling I imagine it'll be a piece of cake.'

'Certainly I feel more confident now, but I shall be glad when it's all signed and settled,' Joanna said. 'I don't want to share with anyone really, but as it's only for a year—unless that's just a ploy to make me agree.'

'Joey!' Julian protested. 'You're so suspicious. If Adam and Kamla say that she's here on a year's contract then why should you disbelieve them?'

'Well, it all seems to have happened in a rush, and Adam appeared to be against women doctors until now, so—yes, I do feel suspicious, and anxious that I'm doing the right thing.'

'It's not the end of the world, Joanna,' Julian said impatiently. 'Agree to a month's trial period.'

'Now why didn't I think of that? That's a great idea—oh, bless you, Julian.' She leaned across the desk and kissed him on his cheek, but it satisfied neither of them and their lips met in sudden harmony, a moment of unsolicited passion which had been absent of late, and then a surreptitious cough made them part.

'Excuse me for—er—interrupting—but it's as well that both

of you are here together as Kamla wants to report the new admission's condition before she goes off duty. Officially it's your case, Julian, but Kamla was eager to get stuck in today.' Adam managed to look disapproving, yet beneath the austere glare he afforded them there was the hint of amusement. 'Go ahead, Kamla,' he invited with a sweep of his hand.

'I've brought my notes personally as I'm going off duty until tomorrow,' she said. 'The young man's name is Wayne Cook, he's twenty-three years old and in deep shock, so he'll be in the shock room for the next forty-eight hours. There are some superficial burns, the blisters have been debrided and dressed with Jelonet, but there are more severe burns affecting the face, hands and trunk. We've put his hands in Flamazine bags following careful swabbing. The main thing to watch is the replacement of adequate fluid both orally and intravenously, otherwise renal failure will occur, but I know the patient is in good hands, Julian.' Kamla's gleaming white teeth sparkled as she smiled at him, and handed over the notes she had made. 'Efforts to reach his parents who live in the Midlands are being made by the police. I hope they will be found, as he needs someone to talk to.'

'Meanwhile,' Adam suggested with a snide glance in Joanna's direction, 'the female staff can do their stuff. A pretty face and warm smile will do much to comfort him—but of course, you're off duty this afternoon, aren't you?'

'Yes, but I'll see him straight away,' Joanna said with an air of authority.

She was glad to make her escape as she felt guilty that Adam and Kamla had caught her and Julian kissing. It wouldn't hurt him to think that there was still something between them, even if he had decided that Julian and Lynn were made for each other. The more she thought about it the more positive she was that it was an idea he had cooked up along with the steaks sizzling on his barbecue. He was trying to stir things, and only because he wanted her to take pity on Kamla. She determined to keep him in suspense about that, but she was becoming more used to the idea of a match between Lynn and Julian, especially as they were both such nice people. Julian couldn't have used her to get to Lynn as Adam had suggested, because he seemed put out by the suggestion of being attracted to Lynn. Joanna smiled to herself as she went along the corridor. Maybe this was one relationship which did need a little help, but she'd have to be discreet about it. She wasn't going to let Adam know that she agreed with him for once.

The staff nurse on duty was at Wayne Cook's bedside in the shock room, and when Joanna had put on a sterile gown, gloves and overshoes she met Joanna at the door.

'He's rather confused,' she explained. 'The shock is coming out and he can't believe it all happened.'

'I'll stay with him until Audrey relieves me at two o'clock,' Joanna said, and went closer to the young man. 'Hullo, Wayne, my name's Joanna Morris and I'm Day Sister on this floor,' she whispered. 'I'm sorry you've had a fright, but you're quite safe with us now, and there's nothing to worry about.'

His face was ashen, his eyebrows and lashes badly singed, but he opened his eyes and stared almost accusingly at Joanna.

'Nothing to worry about?' he croaked. 'My flat—how much damage? And my girlfriend—she'll wonder what's happened. I . . . I don't want her to see . . .' his voice trailed away as he was overcome with emotion.

'Everything will be taken care of, Wayne. Can I get in touch with your girlfriend to explain?'

With some difficulty he told Joanna that Cheryl would be expecting him to call for her at four o'clock. He didn't want her to see him in the state he was in, but neither did he want her to think he had stood her up. After some minutes of quiet, patient discussion Joanna persuaded him to give her the girl's telephone number in Tullbury and she promised to ring as soon as Audrey arrived.

For the next hour Joanna frequently checked temperature, pulse rate, and the amount of fluid which was being given intravenously, and while at first Wayne was extremely alert, as time passed he became alternately drowsy, restless and confused.

Because of the necessity of the large shock room being maintained at a temperature of up to thirty degrees centigrade, which made it very hot and humid, barrier nursing was done by trained nurses who rotated duties every two to three hours. It was well after two o'clock when Audrey Garrett arrived to take over from Joanna.

'He's calmed down a little,' Joanna explained. 'The police are trying to trace his parents, so hopefully they'll be able to get here soon, and I'm going to telephone his girlfriend. He has spasms of being upset and wanting to get up and run, but that's normal. Anything can happen during the next forty-eight hours. Kamla, our new doctor, did the tracheostomy soon after admission as Wayne appeared to have inhaled a fair amount of smoke while trying to put the fire out himself. At first there didn't seem to be too much oedema, but since I've been here his face has swelled considerably. Julian is on duty if you need him; he'll be keeping an eye on him anyway as Kamla has gone off with Adam.'

'Mm . . . like that, is it?' Audrey said. 'Maybe our woman-hater is softening after all.' She turned her attention to the patient. 'I'll take over here until four o'clock and then Simon will be on duty, so Wayne might be pleased to have a male nurse to tend him for a while.'

'Hope it all goes well, poor chap,' Joanna whispered as she opened the door. 'See you in the morning.'

She took off her gown, gloves and overshoes and after checking with Mary, the staff nurse who had covered for her, she went into her office and closed the door. She dialled the number Wayne had given her, but there was no reply. Joanna looked at the clock and saw that it was well past three. He had said that he was due there at four, so Cheryl must soon return. Every few minutes she tried the number again, and then at last a breathless voice answered.

'Wayne, you knew I was going to Mum's for Sunday lunch.'

'Er—Cheryl?' Joanna said cautiously. 'I'm afraid this isn't Wayne.'

'Oh! Sorry, who are you?'

'I'm Sister Morris from Ampfield Burns Unit. Wayne is all right, but he's been involved in a fire at his flat,' Joanna said slowly.

There was a momentary silence, then the questions came think and fast. 'If only he'd come out to lunch with me,'

Cheryl cried. 'Is he badly hurt? Can I see him? Is the flat damaged? Oh, my poor darling—I *must* see him. What about his parents? Has anyone told them? They'll be so worried!'

'I think you'd better sit down for a few minutes, Cheryl,' Joanna advised. 'I realise this has come as a shock to you, but Wayne was concerned that you should be told at once, but on the other hand he doesn't want you to see him like he is. It doesn't look nearly as bad as he imagines and I think a visit from you would be helpful, if you feel you can take it. I don't know how far away you live, but if you could come in today . . .'

'I'll come at once, of course I will—but have his parents been told?'

'The police deal with that kind of thing, so hopefully by now they know and will be able to travel to see him.'

Joanna sensed the hesitation. 'His father is in a wheelchair,' Cheryl said solemnly. 'Wayne's an only boy and came here to get work. He's been doing so well in his job, and we've been saving to get married, then we were going to try to persuade his parents to come here to live. I don't know how they'll manage to get here—and I don't know which to do first, get in touch with them, or see Wayne.'

'I'm afraid I'm going off duty now, but the staff here will do all they can to help you. Take you time, though. Make yourself a cup of tea before you come rushing into Ampfield, and take a few minutes out to think about things. By the time you reach him, Wayne will be feeling more able to communicate and together you can decide what to do about his parents. I'm sorry to have to give you bad news, but it could have been worse, there's always a bright side, and I can assure you that Wayne is going to be all right.' Even as she said it Joanna kept her fingers crossed. She must give the impression of hope, wasn't that what they all survived on? Adam was good at giving his patients and their families hope, and at Ampfield they prided themselves on giving the best care in the world as well as support to the patients' families. She returned to the shock room and through a crack in the door told Audrey to assure Wayne that Cheryl had been told of the accident and would be visiting. All the necessary details would be included in her report, and then she might as well go home as there was nothing more she could do.

Before she went downstairs, though, she looked through the window of the Intensive Care Unit at the King family. Matthew was missing, and where he usually sat at his father's bedside only Mrs King was keeping vigil. Joanna felt a curious pang of sympathy for little Matthew. He was bright-eyed and intelligent, according to Miss Bennett, yet she couldn't help but remember the sad twist of his mouth when she caught him unawares. She went straight to the children's ward and to her surprise found Matthew's elder sister sitting beside his bed. His breathing was being troublesome again—what could be happening? Was his sister unsettling him? Joanna wondered. She put on an air of casualness as she walked though the ward to where Matthew's bed was.

'Hullo,' she greeted him cheerily. 'Bit tired, Matthew?' She raised her eyebrows towards him and he tried to smile bravely. 'Been overdoing it, have you? Breathless again?'

The fifteen-year-old girl turned round to face Joanna. 'He's been crying,' she said. 'Mum wouldn't let us sit with Dad this afternoon. She said I could visit Matthew while she sits with Dad.'

Joanna put a gentle hand on the girl's shoulder. 'It's understandable that they want some time to be alone together, but you can change over presently. Your mother can sit with Matthew while you visit your father—how's that?'

'Mum won't like that,' Sandra said dismally.

'I think Matthew should take it easy for today, so I'll tell Staff Nurse to get your mother to visit him here at teatime, then you can go and talk to your dad.' She looked at Matthew. 'Cheer up, young man, you'll have your dad all to yourself again tomorrow—that's if you're breathing better.' She gave him a saucy wink and he managed a faint smile in response. She would have to sort out whatever Matthew's problems were tomorrow, and she knew that she could count on Adam to help.

When she finally managed to get off duty she called into the Outpatients and accident and emergency department to see Lynn, whom she found alone in one of the small treatment rooms.

'Hi there, Lynn. I'm just off.'

'Lucky you!'

Joanna detected a slight hint of irritation in her friend's voice.

'Had a hard day—after the night before?' Joanna said, trying to sound cheerful.

'Busy, but it's quietened down now, thank goodness.'

'Yes, poor old Wayne Cook. He's in a bad way.' Joanna noticed that her friend was only answering in crisp monosyllables, and it was unlike her to be uninterested, she was usually lively and talkative, but she did look pale and worried. 'Is anything wrong, Lynn?' she pursued.

'No. Why should there be?'

'You aren't your usual happy self. Everything all right at home?' Joanna knew that her mother disliked being left for long periods alone at night when Lynn was not working.

'Everything's fine—just tired, I guess.' It wasn't an answer, just an excuse to shut Joanna up. She tried again.

'You're off at six, aren't you? How about bringing your mum over for a meal? A very light one, that is—I don't think I'm up to creating anything very appetising today.' When Lynn didn't reply Joanna peered into her friend's face. 'What's wrong? You know you can't fool me. Has something happened?'

'Mm . . . nothing serious, Joey, it's just me being selfish and stupid.'

'Can't you tell me about it?'

Lynn glanced almost guiltily at Joanna. 'You least of all, but don't worry—it's really nothing. All I need is plenty of hard work and a good night's sleep. Tomorrow is another day. I should think you need a long night of rest too.'

'Yes, some party, wasn't it? I was surprised to find that Julian left without me. I didn't want Adam to have to take me home. We only quarrelled again about Kamla coming to stay at Willow-Weed, but—well, she is rather nice, isn't she?'

Lynn actually smiled. 'So he's getting his own way after all?'

'Julian suggested the sensible thing, which I wish I'd thought of, and that is to agree to her moving in on a month's trial period.'

'Oh, good old Julian, always first with free advice.'

'Don't tell me that he's upset you?'

'No—no!' But Lynn's expression did not inspire confidence.

'Oh well,' Joanna said, deciding that she was wasting her time, 'I'll get off home and leave you to it.'

'Joey, I'm sorry,' Lynn apologised. 'You're right, I suppose I am tired today. Thanks for the invitation, but there are a few things I ought to do at home. You know how it is?'

'It's Sunday, and your mother takes exception to you doing housework on Sundays, so no, I don't know how it is, but evidently it's a bad day and you'd rather not keep me company at Willow-Weed, so I'll rest alone with my turbulent thoughts.'

'Sorry, Joanna, really I am, but I've got enough of my own turbulent thoughts for the moment.'

'You know where I am if you want to talk, Lynn. Maybe when you get home you'll change your mind and you know you're very welcome if you do. Love to your mum. 'Bye for now.' And Joanna went on her way with a puzzled frown creasing her brow.

Yesterday Lynn had been quite happy. Adam had said that she and Julian had gone off together after the party compatibly enough, so what had happened to change things? She couldn't remember when she'd seen Lynn so down, and she was worried. Perhaps Mrs Dalton was being awkward. Maybe there was something about Julian she didn't like, though Joanna couldn't imagine what—and it wasn't characteristic of Lynn's mother to find fault with any of the staff at Ampfield. Joanna sighed as she drove away from the hospital and through the country lanes to Willow-Weed. She hated discord, especially when it concerned her closest friend, but if Lynn didn't want to confide in her then there was little she could do about it. She had said she had turbulent thoughts, but for the first time in days she felt less fraught. Willow-Weed was to be hers, her very own cottage, and she was to have a companion for a while. When she opened her front door and went inside she tried to imagine what it was going to be like to be able to talk to Kamla, to share the kitchen—no, that might not be so easy, but they'd manage, she supposed. Taking turns in the bathroom could also be a problem, but she must not look on the black side. She would have the pleasure of seeing Adam during his off-duty hours—but he would have eyes only for the beautiful Indian girl. Wasn't that going to be agonising?

Joanna was glad to get out of her uniform, but she put off having a bath until later when she had tidied her bedroom and lounge. By six o'clock it was obvious that Lynn wasn't going to come with her mother, so Joanna made a pot of tea, toasted some sandwiches and made herself comfortable in the lounge in front of the television. The hymn-singing programme came from a seaside town up on the north-east coast and she enjoyed it, but afterwards she felt sad for no reason in particular—except that she was worried about Lynn. She experienced a strange feeling that something or someone had come between them, and it could only be Julian, but why? she asked herself. She thought that she had settled the extent of her friendship with him once and for all, and it had made her feel temporarily satisfied, but now there was a growing feeling of unrest. Julian had made remarks about marriage—Lynn was clearly unhappy—and yet Adam had suggested that Julian was interested in Lynn. There didn't seem to be a problem—Joanna couldn't, wouldn't believe it was Mrs Dalton who was opposed to their friendship, so who else was there who could possibly be raising objections? A weird feeling came over her that she was in some way to blame—but why? How? There was only one solution, and that was to face Julian with the problem. He had helped her over many a hurdle, at least she felt they could be honest with one another.

CHAPTER SEVEN

NO OPPORTUNITY arose for several days during the following week when Joanna could speak to Julian in confidence. The wards were busy, and in her off duty Joanna kept appointments with her solicitor, and the agent dealing with the sale of Willow-Weed Cottage. She should have felt elated, because a very realistic price was agreed upon and all she had to do was to sit back and wait for the contracts to be drawn up, the signing of which, she was assured, would be done at a very early date. But Lynn's smileless expression and downcast appearance took away any feeling of excitement and Joanna avoided too much contact with her friend. In turn it seemed as if Julian was avoiding her.

In less than a week after Adam's party, Joanna had not long been home one evening when she heard the crunch of car wheels on the gravel drive-in from the lane. She peeped from the kitchen window where she was preparing a meal and saw to her horror that it was Adam and Kamla. Now this is just not on, she told no one in particular as she dashed upstairs to change out of her brief shorts and even briefer sun-top to a button-through cotton dress. By this time the doorbell had pealed at least three times, and when she opened her front door Adam didn't wait to be invited in but walked with his usual brisk strides into the hall.

'I thought I was going to have to rescue you from drowning in the bath or something.'

'No,' she answered pertly. 'I haven't been in long enough to do anything but start preparing a meal.'

'Joanna,' Kamla said, 'this is a frightul imposition, but we were both distressed at the state of your clothes after the party, but I'm pleased to say your dress at least has come to no harm, so I wanted to return it to you as soon as possible.

We went to the ward, but they said you'd left an hour before.'

'So, as Kamla tells me you'd invited her here to see the cottage where she'll be living, I decided to come straight on here. I was going to suggest we took you out for a meal to compensate for the inconvenience of spoiling your clothes, but if you're already preparing . . .?'

'Yes, I am, and—er—well, it might stretch to three.' Joanna's mind was in a turmoil as she visualised the dish of fish rice salad being shared between three plates. Thank goodness she had prepared the watercress first. It was all she had and it would have to do, she thought truculently. 'Come along in, but I'll have to leave you while I finish preparing.' She led the way into the lounge, then realised that Adam had returned to the car, and in a moment reappeared carrying her dress, freshly laundered, hanging on a hanger and covered with polythene.

'None the worse for its ducking, along with its delightful wearer, I hope,' he said, smiling broadly.

Kamla handed over a carrier bag in which Joanna found sandals and bag, not the baptised ones, but brand new, still in wrapping from the same shop where she had bought the original ones.

'Oh, you shouldn't have!' she exclaimed. 'There was no need, the others would have dried out, I expect.'

'They did, after a fashion,' Adam said. 'But they can go to my aunt's jumble sale. Nothing less than perfect to go with the new dress, and if you don't tell your aunt I'm sure she'll never know.' He strode about, looking extremely handsome in hopsack slacks with a blue and white knitted shirt. It had been a heavenly summer's day and both Adam and Kamla looked self-satisfied, so Joanna found herself wondering how they had spent the last few hours. Swimming? Sunbathing? Making love? If only the walls of Portia House could tell her their secrets!

'Perhaps, Joanna, while you're doing whatever it is that's claiming your attention I could show Kamla over the cottage?' Adam suggested.

'Mm, ye-es, but you haven't seen all over it yourself—and there is just one thing, before I commit myself, I think

Kamla and I must agree to a month's trial period—after all, anything can happen—sharing a kitchen for one thing can be a trifle strained.'

Adam looked taken aback. He was just a bit too cocksure of himself, Joanna decided, but his warm, sympathetic glance at Kamla made her aware of just how sure he was with the Indian doctor.

'Of course, Joanna,' Kamla agreed instantly. 'That is a fair arrangement, but I have no fears about us quarrelling in the kitchen.' Her bright smile reached out to Joanna, who pointed the way to the upstairs rooms directing Kamla to the bedroom she would occupy.

'I like the back room overlooking the garden,' Joanna said. 'With my owl for protection, though you'll hear him everywhere during the late evening when he goes hunting for his supper. The front bedroom is larger but just as quiet as we get little traffic up here at any time of day or night.' She returned to the kitchen and by the time they came downstairs again she had set the table in front of the open patio doors and was finishing off her dish, which she carried to the table. For once, she thought, she hadn't been caught too much on the hop, trying out a new recipe and hoping that it would have sufficed for two days, but at least it was good to look at and suitable for an Indian girl.

As soon as they sat down Kamla asked: 'Please? What is this, Joanna?'

'I hope you'll like it,' Joanna said hesitantly. 'It's savoury rice pre-cooked, with a tin of tuna fish added, flaked and mixed in with cooked mushrooms chopped with hard-boiled eggs blended together with some mayonnaise, and of course a small onion. According to the recipe the mushrooms and onions should be raw as it's a health recipe, but I think I prefer to eat them cooked a little.'

Joanna passed round the dish, noticing that Adam served himself with a very modest portion of the savoury fish rice salad, and was rather quiet while he sampled it, but very soon his plate was empty and he held it up for more.

'Can I play Oliver Twist and ask for more? It's very good, Joanna. You'll have to give me a written recipe, so that I can surprise my father and Aunt Vera when they come to supper.'

'It's very simple,' Joanna said. 'I'm glad you like it.'

'It was quite delicious and not harmful for my figure,' Kamla laughed. 'I'm hoping that I shall lose some weight while working at Ampfield.'

'We don't want to rush you, Joanna,' Adam said, 'but when can I help Kamla to move in?'

Over coffee they discussed the necessary details and it was all arranged for the following weekend. After they had left Joanna felt quite lightheaded. It had been pleasant to have company, someone other than Julian, although he was always such a good companion, and thinking of him again reminded her of the tension which she felt had sprung up between them, and between her and Lynn.

When she went on duty after a midday break a few days later Joanna could hear raised voices coming from her office and to her surprise found Mrs King, looking rather angry and red in the face, verbally attacking Julian who looked just as angry.

'It really is nothing to do with you people how we run our lives!'

'Lives, Mrs King, which might have been brought to an untimely end in that fire. Every time you visit you upset young Matthew. Sister Morris here and her staff have worked tirelessly to make him happy, and with a team effort by his visiting his father he was making excellent progress, and your husband too, even though as yet he's unable to communicate.'

'And my husband wouldn't be in that condition if it hadn't been for Matthew. I told my husband that the firemen would rescue him, but oh no, he had to try to be a hero.'

'And he was very brave, Mrs King. I understand that this has all been traumatic for you, but you do seem to shut Matthew out, and when one of our patients is unhappy and his condition regresses it's our job to find out why. Because of the seriousness of the situation I suggest that each of you has a chat with our Dr O'Brien.'

Mrs King snorted her disapproval. 'Matthew only puts on this act of not being able to breathe when I come in. He's well enough to come home now, and then I could visit Ken by myself.'

'Matthew is not ready to be discharged. I think you'd better see Mr Royston.'

'Just see to it that Matthew isn't with his father when I come in.' Mrs King turned abruptly, brushing past Joanna roughly before she hurried down the corridor.

'Whatever's happened?' Joanna asked. 'She's one heck of an angry woman.'

'You can say that again, and Adam is going to be angry too.' Julian sighed. 'Matthew was with Mr King when Mrs King arrived, so she sent him back to the ward by himself, and when Mary found him he was in the corridor crying his eyes out and gasping for breath. We've put him on a ventilator to ease things for the poor little chap. Just for a couple of hours, but that wretched woman is undoing all the good we've done so far. It's she who should see the psychiatrist, and the sooner the better, but she won't, of course, because she's too proud. What do you make of it, Joey?'

'It's more than just jealousy, isn't it? Even more than her blaming Matthew for Mr King's condition. Maybe Dr O'Brien will be able to get something out of Matthew.'

'Well, I've told her that if she continues to upset Matthew then she won't be allowed in the hospital.'

'Bit drastic, wasn't it?' Joanna questioned with a smile. 'Come on, let's have a cup of tea.'

'Oh, Joey, that's the best offer I've had all day. I'm due for a break, so I might as well have it here with you.'

They went along to the ward kitchen where, against all the rules, Joanna made a pot of tea. Mary promised to be their lookout and they sat on either side of the table with time to reflect, but no matter how much they discussed the King family there seemed to be no reason for Mrs King's hostility towards her young son Matthew.

'I'll be having a meeting with Adam later on this evening,' Julian said, 'so we'll see what he suggests, but he's already contacted Dr O'Brien.'

'Julian,' Joanna broached cautiously, 'I know you're going to think I'm a turncoat, but Kamla is coming to share the cottage with me. On a month's trial period, like you suggested.'

She explained how Adam and Kamla had turned up at Willow-Weed with her dress, and the new bag and sandals. 'Adam more or less invited himself to share my meal. It was nice to have company and I feel fairly confident that Kamla and I will get along OK.'

'Oh, that's good. Everything is settled, then, but that means that we'll have to meet out.'

'Don't be silly. Nothing need change between me and my friends, only—well, do you happen to know what's bugging Lynn? She looks really miserable and hardly talks to me. What have I done?'

'You told her about your disfigurement. She feels sorry that she didn't know and she's quite adamant that I should marry you at the first opportunity because you think you're so unattractive to men.'

'That's true enough, but it doesn't affect anyone but me, and of course I wouldn't let you marry me just out of pity.'

'But I wouldn't be marrying you just out of pity, Joey,' Julian said solemnly. 'We've been such good friends I can't imagine life without you.'

'You're very sweet, Julian, and we will always be special friends because of all that's gone before. I couldn't have coped with life without you, but—I'm sorry if this hurts, but I don't love you the right way for a marriage to work.'

'Someone else?'

Joanna was forced to lower her gaze into her teacup where the reflection of Adam's face seemed to shine through the shimmering liquid.

'It's going to be hell, and I know I'm torturing myself because by having Kamla to live with me I shall have to stand by and watch Adam and her together, but at least it's a way of having him near sometimes. Only for a year, though, and then I suppose they'll go off somewhere together.'

'Joey, I didn't realise that you felt quite so intense about Adam. I've seen all the signs of admiration—but then half the nursing staff show those same signs.'

Joanna laughed. 'So? It's infatuation. Now even I feel better. I'm sure I'll get over it, given time—but there's nothing to stop you attaching yourself to Lynn. You and she—well, I can't think why I've only just realised it, but you're made for each other—go on, make her happy, Julian. It would make me happy too.'

'Adam has put you up to this, hasn't he? It was he who suggested that I take her home after his party.'

'That was because he was working on me to get me to agree to have Kamla share Willow-Weed.'

'And he's succeeded, hasn't he?'

'Mm, in a way. If there was any danger of it becoming a permanent arrangement then I wouldn't have agreed, but she's only here for a year and then I suppose they intend to get married.'

'I still think you may be wrong about that, Joey. She's older than Adam, for one thing, and although they share a mutual admiration for one another they don't behave as if they're deeply in love. Besides, if they were, surely there's nothing to stop them getting married now?'

Joanna was thoughtful and remained silent. Julian's suggestion was what she'd like to think was true. She knew he was trying to boost her morale just as he had done on so many previous occasions, but she needed to keep reminding herself that once any man saw her scars he would lose interest at once. Julian's talk of marrying her was his way of treating her kindly. He was the type of man who couldn't hurt anyone, and they had grown into a sharing relationship, but it was not the stuff marriages were made of, and Joanna had done with pretending. She saw the mirrored image of her friend Lynn in the brown liquid which lay unsteaming in the bottom of the cup. It looked flat and lifeless, just as Lynn had looked over the past few days, and Joanna wanted to help.

'We must do something to get Lynn out of her depression,' she said now, hurriedly washing down the remains of her tea. 'She says her mum's all right and she's healthy enough, so it must be an affair of the heart.'

'Stop being so dramatic, Joey! You can't arrange everyone's life for them. I am fond of Lynn, yes, I always have liked her a lot, but I never thought . . .' Julian's voice drifted away fruitlessly and Joanna knew that he wasn't being strictly honest with her now. He always had been before, so this must mean that he was teetering on the brink of a discovery. He stood up suddenly, put his cup and saucer in the sink, then toyed with his stethoscope. 'New feller seems to be making a good effort, doesn't he?'

'Yes. It's just a question of time and care for him. He's keen to get out of here, tries to make out that it's all a storm in a teacup; mainly, I suspect, for the benefit of his parents and girlfriend. When I first spoke to Cheryl on the phone she sounded so bossy and abrupt, but she's great for Wayne, and she's marvellous to his parents.'

'I had a chat with her a day or two ago and she's doing everything she can to help them. It's not often these days that you find a young attractive girl eager to push an elderly man around in a wheelchair.'

'Nurses do it all the time,' Joanna reminded him.

'But she's a cosmetic salesgirl,' Julian said with raised eyebrows. 'Doesn't seem the type—still, you never can tell. I must be off—no one else we need to discuss for the present, is there?'

'No, I'll soon bleep you if I need you.'

'When's Kamla moving in?' he asked as he walked to the door.

'At the weekend.'

'So I can come round one evening before then, perhaps?'

'Of course, though I shall have to do a bit of extra cleaning in readiness, but why don't you come and bring Lynn too?'

'I doubt if she'd come—she still things of us as—together, if you know what I mean.'

'Then you must try to convince her otherwise, Julian.'

Mary appeared at the door at that moment. 'Mr Royston is in the children's ward with Dr O'Brien, Joanna.'

'Oh good! That was quick. Let's join them, Julian.'

It seemed that Mrs King had been getting on the wrong side of everyone, so Adam had wasted no time in contacting the psychiatrist. Matthew King had been doing some lessons with Miss Bennett, but now Dr O'Brien and Adam took him into a quiet room on their own, and Joanna hoped that they would find out the cause of his mother's attitude. But after half an hour they returned to the main ward, though Matthew was laughing and seemed much happier, Adam explained that it had been an introductory session and he would be having frequent consultations from now on.

'Can I go to sit with my dad, Sister?' Matthew asked Joanna with bright eyes.

'Maybe later on, young man,' Dr O'Brien said, ruffling the little boy's hair. 'It's my turn to visit your dad now, and I'll tell you how he is when I see you tomorrow.'

'D'you think he'll talk to you?' Matthew asked.

'I hope he will, Matthew, I very much hope he will, but we mustn't tire him too much, must we?'

Joanna watched Matthew smiling up at the Irish doctor with the implicit trust of a child and with a nod the group of doctors went away in earnest conversation. Julian held back briefly. 'Wait for it, Joey. We're on the way to see you-know-who. Hope it works.'

'Good luck,' Joanna said, and holding Matthew's hand she led him back to the centre table where tea was about to be served.

She would like to have gone up to Intensive Care later on to hear from Audrey how Mrs King had reacted to the psychiatrist, but she was kept busy as at last Mr and Mrs Malvin were being moved to one of the new units. Eight-year-old Elizabeth was ready to leave Intensive Care too, but she needed extra attention, so it was decided to keep her in the main ward while Susie and Anthony could now go to the unit with their parents.

They were very impressed with the large room, which had a smaller connecting room where the two younger children would sleep. They had the benefit of a television, and a bathroom en suite, which seemed a luxurious progression from all the family being in different wards.

'Life will be so much easier for everyone concerned,' Joanna explained to them. 'You only have to buzz if you need a nurse, but you'll all help each other, and of course with children of five and under it's so beneficial to be cared for by their parents.'

'It's been a long hard road,' Mr Malvin said. 'But we're all together and alive, and have so much to thank everyone here at Ampfield for. I only wish there was some improvement in Mr King. It's sad to see him lying there so silent. It's almost as if he doesn't want to wake up.'

'There's more to it than being injured in the fire,' Mrs Malvin said. 'I know it's nothing to do with us, but when you nurses aren't around, Mrs King does nothing but grumble at the poor man.'

'It's possible that the fire has affected Mrs King more than anyone realises,' Joanna said. 'Shock affects people in such different ways, but we're making every effort to help them as a family.'

She had to be as tactful as she could, but so often patients were able to help one another, and sometimes became aware of things not easily observed by the staff. It was too late when she went off duty to visit the Intensive Care Unit, but she made a note of what she'd been told in her report and after handing over to the night staff she went off duty. There was no sign of Lynn in her department, even though there was the usual amount of activity on account of several casualties being brought in, so Joanna drove home and managed to relax by cleaning Kamla's room in readiness for her arrival in two days' time. Joanna had the next morning off, so she slept in for an extra hour and then spent more time making the cottage as attractive as she could, but just before eleven she heard voices in the garden and when she went to her patio doors she found Lynn with her mother admiring the view as well as the garden generally.

'What a lovely surprise!' Joanna said. 'But why ever didn't you ring first, Lynn?'

'We didn't know we were coming, Joanna, and I'm sorry if it's inconvenient. I had to take Mum in to the hairdressers—she's sick of me playing around with her hair—and then she thought she'd like to go to the nurseries in the next village to order two new rose bushes—so as I *know* I owe you an apology I thought we'd pop in for a coffee—if you'll have us?'

Joanna smiled happily. 'You know you're always welcome. Where shall we have it, in or out?'

'Mum can sit on the seat out here in the sun while I come in and help you.' Lynn followed Joanna into her kitchen.

'What's all this about an apology?' Joanna asked.

Lynn touched Joanna's arm lightly. 'I'm a silly fool,' she said in self-accusation. 'I hate having to admit to jealousy, but at Adam's party you seemed to have everyone dancing attendance on you. Why shouldn't you? You're popular—I just don't know what came over me, and yet after what you told me about your accident I felt so wretched for you.'

'Perhaps I shouldn't have told you about that, Lynn,' Joanna said. 'I'd kept it my secret and I really meant it to stay that way, but because we're friends I felt guilty at not telling you. So now you know you can forget it, and it doesn't have to make any difference to either of us.'

'No, I see that, but I didn't realise that you felt quite as strongly about Adam as you apparently do. Julian came round last night and we had a long talk. I thought I was being loyal to you, Joanna, trying to make him see that you and he should marry. I mean, it's been on the cards ever since you came here, everyone expects it, and although I've always envied you I never thought that he was the slightest bit interested in me—not until the night of the party, then—well, our feelings did get the better of us and I felt I'd betrayed you.'

'What are you trying to tell me, Lynn?'

Lynn played with the spoon in the sugar bowl. 'Mum had gone to bed, so I asked Julian to come in for coffee and we—well, got a bit carried away. Then the next day I accused him of two-timing you. Oh, it's all been so silly. We had a blazing row a couple of days later and all I wanted was to see you back together again. But he assures me that you don't love him.'

'I've been trying to get that through that stubborn head of yours for ages,' Joanna said lightheartedly.

'You aren't just saying that, Joanna? I'm sure Julian still loves you really, but he tells me that for you it's Adam or no one?'

'I think I've wanted Adam since the first day I arrived at Ampfield. I didn't realise it for quite a while because like everyone else I assumed that Julian and I would get hitched one day, but it would have been awful to marry him while loving someone else. That doesn't alter the fact, of course, that there's nothing between Adam and myself. He doesn't know how I feel, but I know that he's besotted with Kamla. She's such a nice person, and you and Julian will have to come to support me a lot once she moves in.'

'If you're not happy about it, Joanna, why did you agree to it?'

Joanna sighed. 'Mm. To please Adam mainly, I suppose, then when he suggested Kamla being here might cramp my style with boyfriends, I felt I had to prove to him that I didn't have any. Stupid, I know—but Kamla is a nice woman and I just hope it's going to work. For her and Adam as well as me. I anticipate he'll be around a lot—it's either going to be painful or I shall see the real Adam Royston, and that will cure me.'

'Does anyone know the real Adam, I wonder?' Lynn said wistfully. 'But, Joanna, whatever happens I hope we'll remain friends.'

'Of course we shall. I can't promise that I shall give Julian up to you entirely, not just yet anyway. It'll always be natural for me to run to him in a crisis.'

'Then the two of us will be eager to help.' Lynn hugged her shoulders and sighed. 'I'm half afraid to believe what's happened to me. A week or two back I couldn't even have imagined that Julian and I—well, it just goes to show how strange life can be. I owe you a lot too, Joanna, so thanks.'

'Your mum will think we've deserted her. You bring the chocolate biscuits and I'll carry the tray. It's a real treat to have some summer days to enjoy.'

Even Mrs Dalton appeared to be better for the warmth of the sun, and Joanna guessed that she was delighted to know that Lynn and Julian were getting together. But Lynn wouldn't be drawn into giving away any secrets as to whether they had made any plans for the future yet. It was far too sudden and early, she insisted, and they needed to get to know one another more intimately.

As the days and weeks passed, though, Joanna noticed that all the bridges seemed to have been crossed with ease. They looked radiant whether together or apart, their cup of happiness overflowing.

Joanna wished her own personal life was as content. Kamla moved in to the cottage but was seldom there, and Adam hardly ever called. For Kamla it was all a question of work and study, though occassionally Joanna would get home to find that the Indian doctor had reached Willow-Weed before her and had prepared a meal. As the evenings drew in Joanna looked forward to the time when they could draw the curtains after tea and spend a couple of hours in each other's company watching television or just chatting. She tortured herself with thoughts of Kamla and Adam up at Portia House making wedding plans for the future. Surely when the weather turned colder Kamla would spend more time at the cottage and invite Adam here.

Throughout the summer months the hospital was busy with a constant intake of patients suffering from varying degrees of burns, as well as other injuries such as dog and adder bites, or limbs lost through industrial accidents, all of which Ampfield was well equipped to deal with.

One evening after Joanna had been assisting in the emergency theatre downstairs as she walked across the waiting hall she heard footsteps running after her.

'Sister Morris, wait! Sister Morris!' Joanna turned and saw Roxanne Parkes rushing across the floor.

'Roxanne, how nice to see you!'

Roxanne gave Joanna an enormous hug. 'I just had to come to tell you,' she said excitedly. 'At last, Martyn and I are getting married. The date had to be altered, but only postponed for a month. Isn't it great?'

'That's wonderful news, Roxanne,' Joanna said enthusiastically. 'But why haven't you been to see us before this? You had to come into Outpatients, didn't you?'

'Yes, I was supposed to, but my grandmother was very ill in Portugal, so Mum and I have been there for nearly nine weeks. Gran went to live there when my grandad died nearly eleven years ago. She doesn't like English winters, so she went to a warmer climate for her rheumatism. They thought I'd find someone else while we were there, but I intend to marry

Martyn and no one's going to stop me. Gran decided she
didn't want to die in a strange country, so as soon as she was
well enough we brought her home with us. Mum has her to
fuss over now, so she doesn't worry about me so much.'
Roxanne hardly took time to draw breath.

'But you are sure, aren't you?'

'About Martyn? Of course, and I took a letter from my own
GP to a clinic in Portugal and they checked that everything
was going on all right. Look, my hair is almost back to normal
and I have it specially cut to hide the scars, but even they're
fading, just like Mr Royston said they would. Where is he?
Oh, I would like to see him.'

Roxanne had pulled her hair aside for a second so that
Joanna could see the effects of the skin grafts which Adam had
done with such patience and skill, but her excitement was
hardly contained.

'I've brought your wedding invitations—don't forget you
promised—you did!' she said urgently.

Joanna laughed. 'You haven't changed a bit. Yes, I'd love to
come if I possibly can, but I can't speak for Mr Royston.
We've been busy in theatre, but I expect he'll be out in a
minute.'

They stood talking for a few minutes more, and then Adam
came out of the swing doors in his usual rush. He stopped
short, staring at Joanna, then at Roxanne, and his face lit up.
He held out his arms to the young girl and she ran to him,
spilling out all her news without giving him time to respond.
When at last she stopped Adam let her go and laughed.

'You're going to wear that young man of yours out, you
know. Yes, Roxanne, I promised I'd come to your wedding if I
possibly could, so I'd be delighted.' He took the invitation out
of the large white envelope and read the gold-printed wording
on the elegant card. 'Hmm,' he mused, then turned to Joanna.
'Looks as if this is one occasion we can enjoy together.' He
passed her the invitation to read.

'I'm sorry you're both on it together,' Roxanne said, 'but we
were getting short of cards and Mum thought you wouldn't
want to be bothered coming anyway.'

Joanna looked up at Adam quizzically. Did he really mean

that he would go? She did hope he wasn't raising Roxanne's hopes falsely.

'We'd love to go, wouldn't we, Joanna?'

'I promised Roxanne from the start that I'd go,' she said pointedly. 'Do you think you'll be able to get away?'

'Nothing will prevent me,' he said. Then taking the card back again he added: 'And I'll reply officially on behalf of us both.' He excused himself and hurried away, leaving Joanna somewhat mystified. Surely he'd expect to take Kamla, just as she had anticipated taking Julian with her, but now that wasn't possible, so it was a pleasant thought that she would have Adam all to herself. But later her enthusiasm diminished as she supposed he'd make an excuse not to go at the last minute. But, just in case he did keep his promise, Joanna decided to splash out on something really smart. The wedding was to be in September when the Cathedral would be decorated for the Harvest Festival. With dismay Joanna remembered the artistic display Adam had created in the carpet of flowers, so she thought that whatever she wore wouldn't be to his taste. He might be happy if she wore Kamla's sari, but she quickly dismissed that notion. He'd be still more happy if it was Kamla who was to accompany him.

The following week saw a change at last in Mr King's condition. Mrs King was confined to bed for a few days with a virus, so she was unable to visit, and Matthew was allowed to spend all the time he wanted sitting by his father's bedside, and on some occasions with Dr O'Brien too. One evening Joanna went to the Intensive Care Unit to fetch Matthew back at bedtime and Audrey, sitting alone in the observation room, motioned Joanna to join her.

'Glad you came up,' she whispered. 'We're getting some response. Mr King has acknowledged that Matthew is with him. He's rambling, but at least he's talking, something about a cat. I'm wondering if their cat died in the fire.'

'Maybe Dr O'Brien will be able to find that out on his next visit.'

'I have the distinct impression that without Mrs King

visiting, her husband has decided that life's worth living after all. Dr O'Brien said that Matthew indicated that his mother didn't like him and his dad.'

'I'm sure Mr King will make a more speedy recovery now,' Joanna said hopefully. 'If only we could keep Mrs King away for a while longer it might help. I think I should take Matthew now, though, it's getting late and if he stays up all the others will think they can too.'

Audrey Garrett nodded. 'Yes, but just stop and have a word with Mr King. Every bit of conversation helps.'

Joanna went into the quiet room where she found Matthew sobbing.

'Darling,' she said gently, 'whatever's the matter? Your dad is going to be all right.'

'Nurse? Nurse? Is that the one with the kind voice?' Mr King's voice was still husky from the smoke he had in-haled.

Joanna placed her hand over his. 'I don't know about that, Mr King,' she said. 'I hope we've all got kind voices. I've just come to take Matthew back to the ward now as it's well past his bedtime.'

'My . . . wife . . . is she all right?'

'She's just a bit under the weather, but she'll be back to visit again soon.'

'Matthew—he's upset about his cat—poor Fluff, I tried to reach him, but it was too late. My wife didn't like the cat . . .' Mr King's voice trailed away as he moved his head from side to side.

'I think you'd better rest now, Mr King,' Joanna said. 'You're going to be fine, and there'll be plenty of time to talk later on.'

Joanna took Matthew's hand in hers. 'Better let your dad get some sleep, I think, don't you?'

'I can come again, can't I? Even if Mum comes in?'

'Of course, darling.' She dried his tears away and allowed him to kiss his father goodnight, noticing that Mr King managed a smile at Matthew's velvet touch.

She tucked Matthew up in his bed, gently fondling his cheeks and brow as she said: 'Night-night,

Matthew. You've made progress at last. Isn't that good?'

The little boy nodded, then he threw his arms round Joanna's neck and hugged her, but she felt tears spilling out again. 'I did love my Fluff, Sister, I didn't want him to be burnt, I really didn't.'

'I'm sure you didn't, Matthew, and the firemen would have rescued him if they could.'

'He must have hidden under the bed. He does when he's frightened, especially when the dustmen come. Dad tried to get back upstairs to find him, but he wasn't allowed. He said that the smoke would have put Fluff to sleep. Mum's glad, she hated him.'

'I expect she's sorry now, though. Maybe you'll be able to have another kitten one day when you're all home together.'

'No, Mum won't let us, but when I grow up I shall have as many animals as I want.'

Joanna did her best to calm him before she handed over to the night staff. At least things were coming out into the open now and with Mr King able to communicate Dr O'Brien would surely be able to help them piece their lives together satisfactorily.

It was dusk when she reached Willow-Weed Cottage and she was eager to talk the case over with Kamla as they sometimes did over their last drink before bed, but as soon as Joanna opened the front door she sensed that there was an alien presence. Adam? No, his car would have been outside, or at least she would recognise his voice—there was a stillness which bothered her, but after a moment's hesitation she forced herself to open the lounge door.

Kamla was sitting in one of the easy chairs and in the opposite one sat a dark-skinned man who stood up as she entered.

'Hullo, I didn't realise you had company, Kamla.'

Joanna noticed at once that Kamla didn't appear to be at ease, but she too stood up now and introduced the stranger.

'This is Das, a . . . a friend from back home.'

He was tall by Indian standards, Joanna thought, but his smile seemed genuine as he put his hand in hers. His eyes appraised her with interest and Joanna thought how pleasant he seemed—yet the atmosphere was charged with malevolence. What had she come home to?

CHAPTER EIGHT

TO RELIEVE the tension Joanna went into the kitchen and put the kettle on. There were no signs of a meal having been prepared or eaten, no glasses or cups left out, so she hoped a cut of tea would mellow the situation. It was accepted graciously, but all Joanna learned was that Das was in the south of England for a visit. Conversation was formal and after about half an hour he left. There were many questions Joanna would like to have asked, but Kamla went up to her room without even saying goodnight.

Joanna was worried, but she felt she couldn't pry, and the next morning she had eaten her breakfast and was preparing to leave before Kamla came downstairs.

'Are you not on duty this morning?' Joanna asked.

'I should be, but there are matters which I must attend to. Adam will understand. I'm sorry Das came here. I will see to it that he does not come again.'

'But why, Kamla?' You're at liberty to have your friends here if you want to.'

'I do not wish him to come again. I must be allowed to do my work without hindrance.'

'Is he on holiday in England?'

'No, he has come here to work after being in America for two years. He is an orthopaedic surgeon and highly qualified. He has obtained a very good post in Bath, but that does not mean that he has licence to visit me here.'

Joanna picked up her bag and left the cottage. She didn't understand quite what was going on, as Das seemed to her to be a nice type of person and surely Kamla should have been pleased to have someone from India to visit her. But whenever Joanna mentioned his name she noticed an expression of contempt come into Kamla's lovely dark eyes. Perhaps he was an old suitor from before Kamla's friendship with Adam—and how did Adam react to Das's arrival? Joanna couldn't tell, because he didn't do a round of the wards that morning even though it was his usual day. Julian came instead and through pressure of work didn't stay for coffee as he sometimes did. When Joanna met up with Lynn in the canteen she told her what had happened.

'He's very handsome and tall for an Indian, but Kamla is fairly tall too. Maybe it's the part of India they come from. I'm just wondering what I've let myself in for, if there's some sort of conflict. I wondered if perhaps Kamla's family don't approve of her affair with Adam?'

'Is there an affair?' Lynn asked with doubt etched in her tone.

'It's not obvious, but then Kamla isn't at Willow-Weed very much, so I presume she goes to her own house with Adam. I suppose this whole set-up is just for appearances' sake. Maybe they were prepared for someone to come spying.'

'But you say he's working in Bath?'

'That's what Kamla said. She's always had a sadness about her. Now she's very upset, even angry at Das's arrival. Just so long as they don't involve me.'

'How about coming out with Julian and me for a drink this evening?' Lynn invited. 'That way you won't have to see what they're up to.'

'But it's my home!' Joanna said indignantly. 'Why don't you and Julian come round to the cottage for supper? I'm off at four today, so I've got plenty of time to prepare something.'

'Mm, all right, but I'll have to see what Julian says first, or you can ask him if he comes up to your ward.' Lynn smiled suddenly. 'Are you missing him, Joanna?'

'Well, a bit, I suppose, if I'm honest, but I still see him at work, so not that much has changed. I've had Kamla at home—not that I see her very much either—and Adam hardly ever comes to Willow-Weed.'

'Poor old you. I'm sorry, Joanna, I know we're not a good substitute for Adam.'

'It just goes to prove what I said—that he only took an

interest in me to get Kamla installed in the cottage—maybe
to get her out of this Das's way, and to keep their
relationship a secret. I'm not sure whether Indian people
approve of marriage to Westerners.'

'I had a patient once who was married to an Indian Army
officer, and they were very much Westernised. It depends
on the individual families, I believe. But these days you'd
think it was all right for her to marry an English doctor.
She's getting on a bit, though, isn't she, and Adam is only
thirty-six. It's all speculation, but we'll come and see what
we can make of it all, if Julian can get off duty in time.'

Joanna decided to get a joint of lamb out of the freezer
which she defrosted in her microwave, and then roasted.
She was quite proud of the runner beans she had grown at
the end of the garden, and with roast potatoes and peas as
well she had a good meal prepared when Lynn and Julian
arrived. They joined her in the kitchen where she poured
sherry into three glasses.

'You go on through,' she said, 'as I'm not good at
working in the kitchen with an audience.'

'It looks as if you're expecting half the staff from
Ampfield,' Lynn joked.

'I thought I ought to prepare enough in case Kamla and
Das were here, but it doesn't look as if she's been home all
day.' But even as she spoke they heard a car arriving. 'Oh-
oh! Speak of the—gosh! Adam is with them—what am I
going to do, Lynn?'

'Feed us all—I told you there was enough for an army.'

Lynn and Julian made themselves scarce in the lounge
and Joanna went through into the hall as the others entered.

'Joanna, I'm sorry,' Kamla said. 'I see you have
company.'

'It's Julian and Lynn, but I've cooked for you as well.'

'Maybe for me, but not for two extra men?'

'Lynn has just remarked that I've prepared for the entire
staff at Ampfield, all I have to do is to lay up three more
places.'

'Joanna, please don't include me,' Adam said. 'I just
brought Kamla and Das home, I don't wish to impose.'

'But you can stay, can't you?'

Adam gave her one of his most bewitching smiles and with a lift of his satin-smooth eyebrows enhancing his dark eyes he was easily persuaded. Joanna took the sherry bottle into the lounge and asked Julian to do the honours while she completed the task of dishing up. The atmosphere was relaxed enough now, she thought as they sat round the candlelit table enjoying lighthearted banter, even Kamla seemingly less piqued.

'I must compliment the cook,' Das said as he laid aside his knife and fork. 'A most competent nurse, I understand, and one who can cook.'

'Cooking is my hobby,' Joanna said, thinking that even if her body was imperfect she could always earn a man's compliments with a sample of her cooking.

'Joanna should make some lucky man an excellent wife,' Kamla said.

'I'll second that,' Julian agreed.

'Now I'll go and burn the coffee,' Joanna said mischievously, and she got up to clear the plates and vegetable dishes. In the kitchen she quickly piped fresh dairy cream on the top of the gateau which she would have to confess came from the supermarket, but which she had filled with fruit and cream, and while she was doing that the coffee was perking merrily. She had to admit that things were going very well. As yet no one had made a *faux pas*, but there was still time, she supposed. Not knowing who exactly Das was made things rather difficult as well as the uncertainty regarding Kamla and Adam. But with four doctors present, and two nurses, the topic of conversation quickly centred on Ampfield. Joanna decided to wash up, and in an instant everyone was on their feet, but Adam insisted that he would help Joanna.

'I keep cadging her coffee, and other meals as well, so I'm sure I should help with the chores,' he said.

Joanna wished Lynn had offered, but no one else moved except to make themselves comfortable in armchairs with more coffee.

'I can manage, Adam,' she said as she rinsed off the plates

and stacked them on the worktop.

'I never doubted that for one moment, my dear Joanna, but we haven't had the chance of a chat since Kamla moved in. Besides, thanks very much indeed for inviting me, you'll never know how grateful I am. How are things working out now that the month's trial period is over?'

'All right, I suppose, but Kamla isn't here very often. she's very clean and tidy, almost too quiet, so there's nothing I can complain about.'

Adam clicked his thumb and middle finger together in mock disappointment. 'And you were so hoping there would be, weren't you?'

Joanna rounded on him in a rare show of quick temper.

'No! Of course not . . .' Then she saw the wicked teasing in his eyes and she was forced to smile. 'It isn't easy sharing after being alone for so long.'

Adam threw down the tea-towel and spanned Joanna's slim waist with his hands. Hands which were not only skilful in the work he did of mending people's damaged skin but devastatingly ingenious in arousing her fallow feelings. Sensations which up till recently only Julian could bring to life crazily danced with excitement as he gently squeezed with his fingers and nuzzled his mouth into the side of her neck, finally paralysing her with a passionate kiss just on the most sensitive spot below her ear. She gasped, twisted this way and that, but he had her in his grasp, refusing to release her so that she was forced round to face him. Their eyes locked in mutual provocation, their lips much too close to allow the moment to pass without a coming together. It was a moment of sheer bliss, although Joanna's brain rebelled, telling her that it meant nothing to him.

'You don't have to be alone,' he whispered, 'ever!'

She felt her cheeks burning as she tried to temper the hammering of her heart against his broad chest. She wanted to push him away, but she was wearing wet rubber gloves and he was pulling her closer, and closer, until she could feel the pounding of his heart against her breasts. Fire was tearing through her limb by limb, lower, out of control, and in response to his hardened masculinity she found herself pressing her knees against his. She raised her hands in surrender, not so much that she didn't want to put them around his neck and beg him to love her, but to avoid spoiling his suit with her wet gloves.

'Quite a big heart there somewhere,' he murmured into her hair. 'And if I keep working at it maybe I can melt the ice which burns so painfully against my fire. Don't fight it, darling. You must let yourself go occasionally.' His lips captured hers again, sweet and succulently demanding, until his tongue coiled around hers like a sensuous snake, pulling her very soul to consummate with his. She didn't think she could bear it. If only they were alone so that they could climb the mountain of ecstasy together, shedding any encumbrances which held them back—and then she remembered that she was the one with the biggest encumbrance of them all. Forgetting her gloves, she pushed against his chest.

'No! *No*, Adam, what will the others think?'

Still he refused to release her and she felt the low animal growl which he turned into a sensuous laugh before she managed to free herself from his embrace.

'Another time, another place, Joanna, and we'll finish what we've started,' he promised.

She was about to accuse him of infidelity when Julian strolled into the kitchen, and with great haste she plunged her hands into the lukewarm soapy water. Adam almost dropped a saucer, juggled it to safety, and the moment of desire was lost.

When she dared to face Julian some minutes later he smiled with his mouth but there was a look of aversion in his eyes. Joanna supposed there had been a too long-lasting friendship between them to allow for new ones to take precedence. But he had Lynn now, so why shouldn't she accept a little affection from Adam, even if she did feel that she was cheating Kamla? For Adam it was just a moment's indulgence, maybe because he felt guilty at being the one who has suggested that Julian was interested in Lynn. Not that Joanna agreed that Julian had used her to get to Lynn.

She didn't really think Julian knew himself that he and Lynn were ideally suited, though it was obvious to everyone now and Lynn radiated her happiness. Soon there would be an engagement, Joanna supposed, and then a wedding. There was nothing to prevent them.

First, though, there was Roxanne's wedding to attend, and it had been Adam's proposal that they should go together. She felt a tight sigh in her stomach—and then the wedding of the year would be Kamla's and Adam's! Where Das fitted in with all this she couldn't imagine, until, after everyone has gone home, and she lay in bed staring into the darkness relishing those few stolen moments of bliss with Adam, she wondered if Das was a relative of Kamla's, a representative from her family, come to officially sanction Adam as a suitable husband for her. No wonder Kamla seemed to despise him so!

She slept for a couple of hours and then realised that something had disturbed her. Fear coursed through her veins as it always did and she sniffed for the smell of smoke, but the alarm hadn't gone off. She had every confidence that it worked, because she had tested it to demonstrate to Kamla less than a week ago. The cottage was burglar-alarmed too—but in spite of this Joanna slipped out of bed, put her dressing-gown and slippers on and crept out on to the landing, intending to go downstairs to investigate, but as she passed Kamla's room she heard stifled sniffs—had she developed a cold? Joanna wondered, but then there were definite sounds of weeping. She listened, feeling guilty at prying, wondering what she could do, but perhaps Kamla was ill. She waited for a few more minutes, but instead of the sounds lessening they became anguished cries, and Joanna believed Das must have brought her bad news. She knocked lightly on Kamla's door.

'Kamla? Are you ill? Is there anything I can get you?'

Joanna waited, expecting to be told to go away, but after some minutes had passed she heard the sound of movement and the door opened.

'Joanna, I must apologise,' Kamla managed to say between sobs. 'I did not mean to disturb you, please—do not trouble yourself on my account.'

'Whatever's the matter?' Joanna asked. 'Has Das brought you bad news?'

Kamla pulled her robe from the back of the door and came outside, obviously in deep distress. 'He is the bad news,' she said. 'He will ruin my career—him, and our families.'

Joanna didn't know how to reply without sounding too inquisitive, so she went to the head of the stairs. 'Let's make a cup of tea,' she said. 'You can talk if you want to—but I don't want to appear nosey.'

Kamla followed Joanna down the stairs and while the kettle was heating up Joanna switched the gas fire on in the lounge.

'It always seems dark and cold in the middle of the night,' she said. 'The tea will warm us up.'

Kamla managed to compose herself by the time Joanna carried the tray into the lounge, but she was trembling as she took the cup and saucer from Joanna.

'You probably noticed that I was not pleased to see Das,' she said. 'Our families have had our betrothal arranged for many years, but I wished to become a doctor and to travel. I knew Das a little from family gatherings, although he came from a town some distance away.'

'Your marriage has been arranged?'

'Almost, but not quite. I managed to get my wish to study medicine, and when an opportunity came for me to come to this country I took it gladly, and that's when I met Adam. We became close friends and we often talked of Das because he too was studying medicine, and he went to America thinking that I would follow him there.'

'You—don't love him, evidently?'

Kamla tried to smile. She had such a beautiful face with near-perfect features usually radiating an inner glow which Joanna knew to be from job satisfaction. But now that inner glow was hidden by scars of pain.

'When we are young we tend to rebel against authority, and I had been to a school in Germany for a while, so I realised that other countries do not have arranged marriages

—indeed, not all Indian families follow this custom, but my parents are old-fashioned in this respect. It was expected of me that I should return to my home town, marry Das and have a large family. They cannot understand that I am dedicated to my work. I wish to study, learn, and help to make things better in India and Asian countries.'

'And what does Das think?' Joanna ventured to ask.

'He wishes us to marry. He tells me of a deep love which may have been instilled in him from an early age, but which he assures me has grown into something very real to him.'

'Perhaps, in time——?'

'Our parents on both sides are pressing for this marriage to take place, but I have refused to be dominated in this way—and I shall continue to refuse his proposal. I did not think he would come to Ampfield looking for me. It has been a most painful and embarrassing time. That is why I could not live in Portia House alone, in case he came after me, and of course although it is a lovely place I do not wish to accept it as a wedding gift because I do not wish to marry him. I am grateful to Adam for looking after Portia House for me, and I am so indebted to you for having me stay here in this delightful cottage, Joanna, but I think I shall have to make plans to move away.'

'But you have a commitment to Ampfield for a specified time, I take it?' Joanna said. 'Surely no one can make you marry against your will?'

'No, but it makes things very difficult between the two families. There is honour at stake here, Joanna, and I know I am causing my parents a great deal of anguish. If only they could accept that I am happy doing the job which I have been trained to do. I ask for nothing more. It isn't right that Adam should have one of his staff working under a strain. I want to stay here, of course I do, but it will be very awkward if Das continues to pursue me.'

'He seems so nice—is it——?'

'He is very nice—a very kind man—for the right woman—but that is not to be me.' Kamla sounded adamant. Joanna had been on the verge of suggesting that it was Adam who was in the way of the arranged marriage, but

Kamla had interrupted, which was perhaps fortunate. They emptied the tea-pot and as dawn was breaking through Joanna suggested that they should try to get some sleep.

'Take a couple of aspirins, Kamla,' she advised, 'and sleep on in the morning.'

'I cannot do that, I'm afraid. I shall be working with Adam to do a small skin graft on Wayne Cook's arm and Adam has invited Das to attend. I regret that he did so.'

Kamla got up and hurried back to her room. Joanna felt sorry for her. It was upsetting to see her under such stress, but was she more dedicated to her job than to Adam? Joanna lay awake and watched the sun rise. She felt guilty now that she had allowed Adam to kiss her, and that she had responded the way she had, but it had been Adam who had started it, she told herself.

Das remained in Ampfield for nearly two weeks. Not only did Joanna feel sorry for Kamla but also for Das. As she watched from a distance she believed that Das was genuine in his affection for Kamla. He didn't arrive with bouquets of flowers or boxes of chocolates, he just continued to visit as a friend, and Adam seemed to welcome his presence, while Kamla tried to ignore him.

One afternoon, a violently windy one during which rain threatened, Joanna had done her round of all her patients and was writing up reports of her findings when Dr O'Brien sauntered through the corridor.

'Hello there, Joanna,' he said brightly, with a twinkle in his Irish blue eyes. 'Everywhere seems mighty quiet, so do I take it that you've time for a chat?'

'Always time for you, Dr O'Brien,' she replied. 'Will I make the tea first or after the chat?'

'First, I'd say, then we can drink and chat at the same time.'

Joanna stood up and went to the kitchen along the corridor while the psychiatrist visited the children's ward, coming to a standstill at Matthew's bed, and when Joanna went to find the doctor to tell him that the tea was made she found him perched on Matthew's bed where the two of them were sharing a joke.

Dr O'Brien ruffled the little boy's head and followed Joanna to her private office where they could talk undisturbed.

'Is it about Matthew you want to talk?' Joanna asked.

'Who else, Joanna? A sad little feller, to be sure, but I think all that may be about to change.'

'Oh? What have you been up to?'

'Mrs King is one of those women who shows a tough exterior, but on the inside she's very insecure. She was the one who switched on the electric blanket and forgot about it. She's the one who insists that the children's bedroom doors are shut tight when they go to bed—in this case it was a good thing Matthew's was closed, it probably saved his life, but, for heaven's sakes, the lad is only eight years old and all kids like to hear that someone is about downstairs.'

'And according to Matthew she doesn't like him very much anyway,' Joanna said.

'Aha! An unwanted baby, Joanna—and whereas some women try to make up to the child afterwards by spoiling them rotten Mrs King has felt nothing but contempt for the poor boy. The cat was a bone of contention between her and Mr King and Matthew. She frequently threatened to turn it out, so now that it's died in the fire—from the effects of smoke—she feels guilty about that too. But from the talks we've had, she's feeling better within herself now. She realises that she very nearly lost her husband, although she tried to blame Matthew for that. We've a good way to go, but we're making progress, and I want to see a better attitude to Matthew before he's allowed to go home. He doesn't want to leave hospital as long as his dad is here. He'd have no one on his side, you see.'

'You've analysed them very well, Dr O'Brien,' Joanna said. 'It's been obvious from the start that Matthew was made to feel guilty about his father's condition, and now that Mr King is talking let's hope they'll all be drawn closer together.'

'Mrs King has accepted responsibility—in her heart she knows it was an accident—but it'll take a time before she can change how she feels about Matthew. I think she's going to make an effort, though—and I hope you're going to forgive me for what I've done.' Dr O'Brien raised his eyebrows questioningly.

'That sounds ominous—go on, surprise me.'

'I've persuaded her to go out and buy a kitten. One as near to what Fluff was like as she can. She's to bring it into the ward, wrapped in a blanket, or in a basket, she's to show Matthew that she does like animals.' The doctor chuckled. 'At first she threw up her hands in horror, but I put a cat on her lap, suggested that she close her eyes and stroke it gently. We're finding cats and dogs beneficial in the treatment of the mentally ill as well as geriatric patients.'

'I bet she didn't like that,' Joanna said. 'I'm sure she wouldn't like to hear you include her in either of those categories.'

'When I explained that she needed remedial treatment, that we now use animals for that purpose, she began to listen—and it wasn't easy for such a woman as her.'

'Matthew will be delighted.'

'He'll be told the truth about his cat, and the new Fluff, and we'll let Mrs King do the telling. He'll be anxious to get home after that, I daresay, and as Adam says, there's nothing to keep him here now except that he believes his father needs him. He's an intelligent boy and we've played games to show that each person in a family needs all the other members of the family. He plays a good game of chess too, thanks to his father.'

'It's usually women and their daughters who don't get on—the jealousy thing over the man, but I fancy poor old Matthew would have got a raw deal if it hadn't been for his father.'

'There've been some personal problems between the parents over the years. Mrs King was possessive over the girl, so Mr King found some comfort from his secretary until she married someone else. That's how Matthew came about. Still, they're a nice family and deserve to get the best out of life, and I think they will when they get over this trouble. When they realise how precious life is they'll take care to protect each other. Most of today's problems come about through sheer selfishness, you know, Joanna.'

She agreed, and after Dr O'Brien had left she gave the matter some thought in respect of Kamla and Das. Someone was going to have to give way. Kamla was too old to be made to marry a man she didn't love, and Das would have to give up his quest. Could it really matter what the parents had arranged to a man of his calibre? He was well educated and used to Western ways. He had lived away from his own culture just as Kamla had for some years, so Joanna couldn't believe that Kamla's refusal to marry him just to please the families could be that important to him unless he was genuinely sincere in his feelings for her. Kamla and Adam were being selfish in their relationship and were too blind to see just how keen Das was on Kamla.

Joanna felt annoyed with Adam that he had involved her. She had been quite content to live at Willow-Weed Cottage on her own and be self-sufficient, but now she had an unhappy guest in her home, and even if there wasn't much she could do about it she felt that it reflected on her. She was on duty late that evening, so she ate at the hospital, and after visiting the Intensive Care Unit and making sure all the patients in her charge were as comfortable as could be expected she drove home through a deluge of hailstones. As she ran from the car to the shelter of the porch she almost slipped up on them, but Das opened the front door and managed to support her before she fell.

'What stupid weather!' she grumbled.

Das laughed and held her steady. 'You never know what's coming next,' he joked. 'Tomorrow the sun will be shining again.'

'I hope we shall have a nice September. One of our young patients is getting married at the Harvest Festival weekend.'

'And you've been invited?'

'Yes, and Adam.' As Joanna took off her soaked nylon mac she explained about Roxanne's accident, and Kamla came from the kitchen.

'Have you eaten, Joanna?' she asked. 'There is some of our curry left, but it may be too hot for you.'

'I have eaten, thanks,' Joanna replied. 'But I'm getting used to Indian curries.'

'Come and join us for coffee, then,' Kamla said, and Das went to help Kamla.

As they sat round talking Joanna had the sudden strange feeling that she was an intruder in her own house. The feeling of animosity, which had previously been so evident when these two were together, was absent. What had happened to change things? Joanna wondered. Before Das left, when the storms had passed and an orange sunset illuminated the sky, Kamla accomapnied him outside and from her bedroom window Joanna saw them together talking. Kamla wandered round the lawn, Das a little behind her, and when she stopped he caught up with her and placed his arm comfortingly about her shoulders. Joanna experienced a sickly feeling in the pit of her stomach. She felt guilty at watching, but Kamla's light laugh echoed up to her and she realised that either they were putting on a very good act, or there was some chemistry reaction between them. What was Adam going to make of this? she wondered.

Joanna enjoyed having a couple of days off so that she could shop in readiness for the wedding, and do some odd jobs around the cottage. Kamla's financial help was useful in buying paint for the kitchen which Joanna intended to do a bit later on. It was pleasant to have the cottage all to herself as Das had returned to Bath, and Kamla said she expected to visit him there at the weekend when Adam and Joanna were attending Roxanne's wedding. When Joanna returned to duty little Matthew came running towards her excitedly.

'Sister Morris, Sister Morris—oh, I'm so glad you're back,' he cried enthusiastically. 'Mummy's bought me a new kitten—just like Fluff—you won't mind her bringing it in to see me, will you?'

Joanna hugged the little boy, delighted to see the change in him.

'Of course not, darling,' she said. 'As long as you make sure he doesn't escape. The hospital's rather large and if he gets frightened he might run and hide and we shan't know where to find him.'

'Mr Royston said we could go into that little room at the end of the corridor, then the other children won't see. Just one more time, he said, and then I can go home.'

'That is good news, Matthew. I bet your mum will be pleased to have you home again.'

'She hasn't been very well,' Matthew said solemnly. 'Dad said I must go home and help her now. He's getting better too.'

'It'll be great when you're all home together,' Joanna said, and although she recognised some doubt in Matthew's voice she had the feeling that thanks to Dr O'Brien everything would sort itself out. Pain, as she knew from personal experience, wasn't always physical. Pain on the inside was sometimes much worse—just as she had felt when her parents had returned home after her accident and then gone off again. No matter how kind and loving her aunts had been, her parents' attitude had made her feel rejected, so she knew what little Matthew had suffered by his mother's lack of affection. But later that day when Mrs King arrived at Ampfield carrying a wicker basket she looked a different person.

'I'm sure you won't approve of this, Sister,' she greeted, 'but Dr O'Brien assured me he was going to talk you into agreeing that I could bring Fluff the Second in to see Matthew. I'll take him out to the car again, if you'd rather, and Matthew can see him outside.'

'Whatever Dr O'Brien says goes,' Joanna said with a laugh.

'Not quite,' a stern voice echoed behind them, and Adam came along the corridor. 'I'm still in charge, Sister Morris.' He walked up to her and gave her quite a heavy smack on her bottom.

'Ooh!' Mrs King said sympathetically. 'I'm sure Sister Morris of all people didn't deserve that, Mr Royston.'

Adam shook his head, but stood with his arm round Joanna's waist.

'You wouldn't believe the trouble I have with this one,'

he said. 'And to think I've got to take her to a wedding with
me on Saturday.'

'Sure it's not your own?' Mrs King asked with a wink.

'Mm—doubt if she'd have me,' Adam said, giving Joanna
a squeeze and making her wriggle. 'Still, it might give us
ideas, mightn't it, Joanna?'

'Not me,' she replied adamantly. 'I'm in love with my
job.'

She felt Adam's had slip away from her waist as he took
the cat basket from Mrs King, and the mewing kitten
attracted everyone's attention. Later when Adam and
Joanna had completed a round of all the patients he said: 'It
looks as if things are going to be better between Matthew
and his mother from now on, or do you think it might be an
act to show off to us?'

'It's difficult to be certain,' Joanna said. 'But I don't think
you can hoodwink children. Matthew is definitely much
happier and Mr King is making excellent progress. How
soon will you discharge Matthew?'

'Maybe we'll try him out this weekend. He can return
here on Monday so that we can give him a final check-up. I
don't want to rush things, but I'm anxious to see how he
copes with a few days at home with the option of returning
here. Hopefully everything will be better than he imagines
so that he'll want to stay with his kitten. Once Mr King sees
that things are all right he'll soon want to go home as well.
It's a great pity that it takes something as serious as a fire in
the home to bring everyone to a better understanding.'

'Talking of better understandings,' Joanna said
hesitantly, 'Kamla seems to be more kindly disposed
towards Das, I've noticed.'

Adam raised his eyebrows significantly. 'They're of the
same culture and background, they share the same
profession—who knows?'

'I think,' Joanna said pointedly, 'that you've used me,
Adam. Setting Kamla up in my home has given her and
Das the opportunity to get to know one another. All in your
little scheme, I suppose?'

'I can't imagine what you mean,' he said, and with an

arrogant swing turned to leave, then he came back to stand very close to Joanna. 'I'll pick you up at eleven-thirty on Saturday. You'll have the cottage to yourself for the weekend, won't you? And I shall have Portia House to myself—your place or mine?'

'*I* can't imagine what you mean!' she retorted cheekily. 'But I'll be ready—I mean for the wedding,' she added hurriedly, and at his meaningful grin she went to put the Kardex trolley away quickly to hide her blushes.

The weekend seemed to be significant for everyone, she thought. Matthew going home with his mother; Kamla and Das spending it on their own, she and Adam celebrating Roxanne's marriage to Martyn and several patients being discharged. When she visited the Malvin family, though, she was reminded that not everyone could rejoice. Eight-year-old Elizabeth's progress was pitifully slow and this was holding her parents back considerably. They were all together in their unit, which was a help to the two younger children, and less stressful for Mr and Mrs Malvin, but they should all have been discharged by now. Joanna had a sudden inspiration and decided to find Matthew and his kitten. It might interest Elizabeth, who was about the same age as Matthew.

It took a little while to track Matthew and his mother down, but eventually she found them sitting together in the back seat of the car in the car-park where the kitten could come out of the basket.

'Matthew, hold on to Fluff,' Joanna called through the window. 'Would you like to bring him back inside? There's someone I'd like you to meet.'

Matthew pushed the small bundle of mischievous fur into the basket and Joanna led the way round to the south side of the hospital.

'You can go to see your husband if you like, Mrs King,' Joanna suggested. 'I'll return Matthew to you in a few minutes.'

Mrs King went inside and up in the lift to the men's ward while Joanna took Matthew and his kitten into the large airy ground floor room where the Malvin family were sitting in the big picture window. Elizabeth was lying in a recliner chair looking pale and uninterested, but when Joanna put Fluff on to her lap she automatically put out her hand to touch him.

'Isn't he cute?' she said in a husky voice. 'I've never had a kitten.'

'Fluff is very special, Elizabeth,' Joanna explained. 'He's replacing Fluff Number One who went to sleep in the fire and wouldn't wake up.'

Matthew jumped in at once with graphic details of the fire at his home, which prompted Elizabeth to talk about her family's experience.

'If it's all right with you, Mrs Malvin. I'll leave Matthew here for a few minutes. As long as all the doors are kept closed the kitten can stay as well.' Joanna went away, hopeful that she had done the right thing, but children could usually elicit a response in one another, she had found from past experience. When she saw Lynn and Julian in the canteen later on she told them of her success.

'When I went back to fetch Matthew and the kitten,' she said, 'Elizabeth was up and chasing round after Fluff, who'd got himself firmly hidden under a chest of drawers. The two youngsters were having a high old time. We had to use a piece of Mrs Malvin's wool to entice him out.'

'It's a pity that Matthew is going home just now then,' Lynn said.

'But it means, my sweet, that we shall have a fairly quiet weekend with so many patients being discharged.' Julian lifted Lynn's chin with the end of his fork.

'Don't bank on it,' Joanna said. 'If the weather is good then it means the world and his wife will be out making the most of it—and that means accidents.'

Julian threw Joanna a mock punch. 'No need for you to be so smug just because Sir is accompanying you to the wedding. Don't go and get hitched by mistake, will you?'

'Just what the doctor ordered, eh, Joanna?' Lynn quipped.

'Dreams—nothing but idle dreams. Still, I'm looking foward to seeing Roxanne all dressed in white. She'll look stunning, and the Cathedral is a lovely place to be married in.'

'Where's the reception being held?' Julian asked.

'At the Tullbury Arms Hotel. All rather grand.'

'Top hat and tails affair?'

'But of course. Mr Parkes is a prominent business man in the city and a councillor as well, so—nothing but the best, even if poor old Martyn was shipped off to Saudi for a while.'

'Roxanne seems to have got her own way in the end, though.'

'By threatening to go to Saudi herself, I understand,' Joanna laughed. 'Maybe she's not so immature after all. I hope their marriage will be a success. I'm quite looking forward to the wedding.'

'Well, don't forget us slaving away while you and Adam go and enjoy yourselves,' Julian said.

'It's not often that Adam can be persuaded to do anything as exciting as going to a wedding. Maybe he wants to see how it's done in readiness for when he and Kamla get married,' Lynn said.

This thought depressed Joanna, and any thoughts she had conjured up about Kamla and Das becoming fond of each other were dashed to the ground. As she drove home that evening she reflected on Lynn and Julian too. They were idyllically happy, and although Joanna was pleased for them she felt sad for herself, tortured by the fear that Lynn might be right about Kamla and Adam. But, come what may, she had the opportunity of having him all to herself on Saturday, so she'd jolly well make the most of it!

Rain clouds came and went early on the morning of the wedding, but by ten-thirty the sun had come out, making everything steam merrily. Adam had driven Kamla to the station the evening before to go to Bath, so Joanna had the cottage to herself and could get ready at her own pace. She bathed and washed her hair, ate a hearty breakfast, knowing that it might be mid-afternoon before the wedding breakfast could begin, and then with just the hairdryer and a styling brush she made the best of her wayward brunette waves.

She paraded in front of the long mirror after she had put on her lacy bra, brief pants and suspender belt. Then she almost held her breath as she rolled on some expensive sheer silk stockings in a shade of midnight blue to match the crêpe silk dress with its twirling skirt and tight-fitting bodice. It had a satiny hexagonal shape woven into the material which glistened in certain lights. Black bag and gloves matched her black velvet jacket, but her high-heeled shoes were dyed blue to match her dress. She had considered getting a hat, but she didn't usually wear one, and after all she was only a guest. She felt very 'dressed-up', and was hoping she hadn't overdone it when the doorbell sounded.

She opened the door just as Adam was about to ring again.

'I thought you'd gone without me,' he said, then, looking her up and down, he made a circle with his thumb and forefinger as he whistled in appreciation. 'I hoped you'd surprise me and be wearing the sari Kamla gave you.'

'I would never dream of doing anything like that,' Joanna replied indignantly. 'I'm very British.'

'I know, darling, but the sari suited you so well. You don't have to be Indian to wear their costume. Women who work in India and Asia often wear saris because they're light and airy in such a hot climate.'

'Have you worked abroad, then?' she asked, picking up her gloves and bag.

'Yes, I went to Tibet, worked there for a year and then made my way home via several other countries. A very special experience.'

'And is that how you met Kamla?'

'That's right. In a children's hospital in Delhi.' Adam moved away from the front door so that Joanna could close and lock it. He walked ahead of her to the car and she noticed how elegant he looked in his dark suit. He always looked immaculate, whether going to a conference or a ward round, but today Joanna could see that his suit was an expensive, well-cut tailor-made one. He reached inside the car before he allowed Joanna to get in, and produced a box covered with a cellophane lid, inside which were two beautiful gardenia buttonholes.

'I know we're not part of the bridal party, but I thought we might as well look the part, and I've remembered some confetti as well.'

'Yes, I bought some paper rose petals, but I didn't think we need bother with buttonholes.'

He opened the box and held the creamy-white gardenia against Joanna's lapel. 'Are you going to keep your jacket on all the time?' he asked.

'I may do, or I may take if off at the reception. Adam, I'm not that keen on weddings—we can come away as soon as the meal is finished, can't we?'

'And you were the one who thought I should make exceptions for Roxanne, which I'm doing. It isn't usual, you know, for consultants to mix socially with their patients, or ex-patients.' Adam stooped to kiss her lightly on her mouth, then stood back and smiled. 'Mustn't spoil your make-up—no, Joanna, we are not going to leave until I say so.'

'It isn't usual,' she said cuttingly, 'for consultants to be seen outside the hospital with other members of the staff.'

'Ah, but it is. People who work together have a way of meeting, falling in love and even marrying. Today, my darling Joanna, we're guests at Roxanne's wedding and we're going to enjoy ourselves, in spite of everything.'

Joanna wondered what the 'everything' was meant to imply, but she looked away as he fastened the buttonhole on her jacket lapel, then asked her to fix his. Adam didn't turn his head. He kept his dark eyes firmly scrutinising her expression and flushed cheeks. She always experienced a cold, tight feeling in her stomach when she was going anywhere, but now she felt again the warmth in the pit of her stomach at his nearness and the masculine smell of him. The blood was flowing much too rapidly through her veins and she was all fingers and thumbs, but finally she managed to secure his white gardenia.

'Thank you,' he said pointedly, holding her firmly

against him.

'Thank you, for the buttonhole,' she said in a low voice, at which he kissed her again, believing her fluttering eyelids were an invitation to do just that.

'Better get going,' he said, and Joanna slid into the front passenger seat of the low-slung high-powered car.

It took about twenty minutes to reach the Cathedral and then came the problem of parking, but it seemed that Adam had already thought this out, as he drove into the narrowest of lanes nearby where no-one else had parked.

'It is all right to park here?' Joanna asked in surprise.

'Indeed it is. I have permission from the clergyman who lives in the cottage there.' He nodded towards the end of the lane as he unfastened his seat belt. 'Do we leave their gift until we get to the reception?'

'Yes. I suppose we should have delivered it earlier,' Joanna said.

'In some countries, Greece for example, the guests take their presents to the church and the bridesmaids accept them at the entrance. But I expect a lot of people will take them to the reception here.'

Adam locked the car up, checked that their buttonholes were still in place and with his arm under Joanna's elbow guided her through a narrow footpath which brought them out directly into the Cathedral grounds. The bells were pealing out across the close and as they approached the open door of the Cathedral a photographer took a picture of them and then a newspaper reporter requested their names.

'You're going to be famous,' Adam whispered.

'My name won't mean anything to anyone,' Joanna said. 'But yours might.'

'And coupled together they can give the gossips something to mull over.'

'I expect most people have got better things to do than gossip about us,' Joanna whispered back frantically.

An usher gave them a printed order of service each and showed them to some seats on the left-hand side of the Cathedral about half-way down. Joanna was delighted to see so many people in the congregation, even on Martyn's side, and while they listened to the organist playing some appropriate music Joanna admired the Harvest Festival decorations. An enormous harvest loaf depicting a sheaf of corn took pride of place, surrounded by fruit, vegetables and a grand display of flowers, and when the bridal procession proceeded to the front Joanna saw that the chosen colour scheme complemented the Festival colours of brown, orange and cream. Roxanne looked resplendent in a billowing cream dress with heavy veiling fastened to her orange-blossom headdress, which cascaded down to her waist, edged with tiny velvet bows. The hem of her long dress and train was also edged with tiny velvet bows and she carried a magnificent bouquet of chrysanthemums in cream, orange and bright yellow. Two adult bridesmaids wore dresses made of donkey brown velvet, decorated with cream lace and bows, while the small pageboy and four-year-old bridesmaid wore cream with brown velvet trimmings.

Joanna willed herself not to shed any tears as she usually did at weddings, but self-pity that she could never be a bride caught in a lump in her throat. Her eyes burned uncomfortably until she was forced to blink back the tears, and as she clutched at the pew in front for support Adam placed his hand protectively over hers. She had hoped he hadn't noticed, but his job was to observe and she guessed that he had sensed the emotion she was feeling. But, she thought, he would never know why her turn to go down the aisle as a bride could only ever be a girlish dream. She fought against imagining how it would feel to stand beside Adam, their relatives and friends in support behind them as they exchanged their vows, just as Roxanne and Martyn were doing now in youthful unashamed vigour. Martyn was a tall, lanky young man with a shock of gingery-blond hair, a fresh complexion and honest pale blue eyes. Yes, Joanna thought, as she witnessed the intimacy of their exchanged vows, Roxanne did love her Martyn in all sincerity—now—but would it last? Would the pressures of modern living with all the commercial aspects be too much for them to weather together?

By the time the bridal party went through to the vestry for the signing of the register Joanna had glimpsed Mrs Parkes dabbing at her eyes. Only those who had seen Roxanne at the time of the accident could marvel at her appearance now and the miracle Adam had performed. But for the prompt action of the emergency services first and then the team at the Burns Unit headed by Adam, Roxanne might not have survived to reach this happy day which Joanna knew was filled with thanksgiving.

Not so for herself. Her scars were hidden from public view but were there as a hideous reminder of youthful carelessness. She would always know how imperfect her body was, and an involuntary shiver over which she had no control tormented her. Beautiful clothes could cover the imperfections, but at the memory of what she saw in the mirror a pain seared down her side just as if she were being scalded.

CHAPTER NINE

DURING the signing of the register a choirboy sang *Ave Maria*, which gave Joanna time to compose herself. She knew that Adam glanced at her from time to time, but when the bridal pair walked arm in arm down the aisle with radiant smiles in all directions she thought they were just faces in the congregation until Roxanne and Martyn reached level with them, and then Roxanne let go of Martyn's arm and reached up to kiss Adam first, then Joanna.

'I'd have died if you hadn't been here,' she whispered. 'It's thanks to you both that I'm alive.' Maybe she saw the fresh tears which flooded Joanna's eyes, and Adam's embarrassed smile, but she carried on with her new husband, amidst smiles and many congratulations out into the autumn afternoon.

As is usual at weddings there were minutes of confusion as guests tried to leave by various means while the frustrated photographer endeavoured to achieve that for which he was being paid. Joanna sat down in the pew again and repaired her face discreetly while Adam looked on with an amused expression.

'Do weddings always have this effect on you?' he chided.

'Mostly,' she answered with a smile. 'It isn't often we get acknowledgement at a wedding. She's a sweet girl and she looks lovely.'

'I've never known a bride yet who didn't look lovely on her wedding day,' Adam said, and then they were swept along with everyone else, eager to watch the proceedings and throw confetti as the couple left for the reception. Joanna ran after them to throw her rose petals, and a gust of wind played havoc with her full skirt, which seemed uncontrollable. One or two men standing around gave wolf whistles as she tried to hold her skirt in place and she was relieved when Adam caught up with her.

'You can tantalise me any time, Joanna, but not half the male population of Tullbury,' Adam said fiercely.

'I couldn't help it,' she protested. 'The wind blew suddenly and got underneath my skirt.'

Adam looked down into her upturned face with smouldering eyes.

'Don't tempt me—yet. Come on, let's get to the car before I make an ass of myself.'

Joanna knew he was only joking, something he did much more of these days, she noticed. It didn't seem so long ago that he appeared to most people as being a killjoy. The Godfather who concerned himself about the welfare of his staff but was far too preoccupied to take part in any social activities, yet now here she was attending a very special function with him. Who or what had caused Adam to change, to be more aware of what was happening around him? Joanna recalled that it was from the time of the barbecue party at Portia House when Kamla had first put in an appearance that everything had changed.

The lane was deserted when they reached his car. He opened the door for Joanna but held her fast before she could get in, and to her horror he tipped a heap of confetti down the front of her dress.

'Oh, Adam!' she complained bitterly, trying to shake it through. 'I shall be dripping confetti wherever I go!'

'And I shall have great fun retrieving it all when we go on to our own party.' Adam indicated that she should get in the car quickly. He was renowned for being an impatient man, but by the flame of lust she saw burning in his eyes she was wary of what he was impatient for at present. But at the reception he was the soul of discretion, a perfect gentleman who complimented Roxanne and her husband to make them feel very special, and in the event Joanna couldn't have wished for a nicer companion on a most happy occasion.

The sit-down meal was delicious, well presented and served by pleasant young waiters and waitresses, and after

the toasts with champagne and a few short speeches there
was a time for general conversation while Roxanne and
Martyn circulated among their guests.

'Can we soon go now?' Adam asked.

Joanna laughed up at him. The fruit punch, which really
did have a punch, followed by wine with the meal, and now
champagne, had helped her to forget that Adam's new
image had been brought about by the arrival of Kamla. She
wondered how they were spending the weekend in Bath,
and if Kamla would be successful in obtaining her release
from the bondage their families had subjected them to.

'You've been very good up to now,' Joanna told Adam.
'You can't disappoint Roxanne. She'll want to see you
before we leave, and you'll probably get another kiss if all
this drink has affected her the way it seems to have everyone
else.'

He turned in his chair and placed his arm on the back of
hers to whisper in her ear. 'It isn't just the wine. You can't
put me in this devastating postion, Joanna,' he said. 'I want
to go somewhere where I can kiss the prettiest girl in the
room—a girl who's much more mature than I'd imagined.
Besides, I need that confetti.'

'Don't be silly,' she scolded. 'Why?'

He breathed heavily for a second and then with a wicked
smile said: 'So that I can do it all again.'

'I think we must make for the nearest coffee shop.'

Roxanne was wending her way to reach them and with an
arm round each of their shoulders she thanked them for the
lovely gift which they had given her, and which Adam had
suggested, which was a fish fryer.

'Hopefully you can't do any damage with that,' Joanna
laughed.

'I wouldn't count on it,' Roxanne returned. 'It'll be safer
than a chip pan, but I'll never use one of those again.'

'I should hope not, young lady. You're looking quite
beautiful, so make sure you stay that way.'

Roxanne planted a very firm kiss on Adam's cheek.
'Thanks for coming. I'll never be able to thank you enough
for all you did for me. You will come on to the house to see

the presents, and then there's a disco here this evening.'

'I don't think . . .' Adam began.

'We'd love to, wouldn't we, Adam?' Joanna said enthusiastically. Adam might have made certain ribald suggestions, but knowing him Joanna expected that he was eager to get back to work, so by accepting Roxanne's invitation she was doing her best to make the day last. 'Aren't you going away?' Joanna asked.

'Oh yes, on the night flight to Italy. Dad has given us our honeymoon, and then we shall come back here for a month before we go out to Saudi together. Martyn likes it there and he has a good job. The money out there is fabulous, so we've decided to go there for at least a year, probably two or three. I'm very excited about it, but my parents aren't too thrilled, but I've told them they'll soon get over it and they can enjoy a second honeymoon without me around.'

'Roxanne, you're incorrigible!' Joanna said.

Mr and Mrs Parkes joined them and after a brief exchange moved on to chat to more of their relatives and friends.

'Let's go and get some more coffee from the lounge, or a cup of tea would be nice,' Joanna suggested.

Adam stood up and moved Joanna's chair out for her. 'I won't forget this in a hurry,' he ground out between gritted teeth. 'Presents, idle chit-chat, a disco?'

'Don't be such an old grumps, Adam. It's Roxanne's day and she's keen for you to enjoy it with her.'

'Well, you're the one who's going to regret it. I had other plans, but we've got all night and all day tomorrow.'

'I'm sorry, Adam, you should have said,' Joanna apologised naïvely. 'I didn't know you'd made other arrangements?'

She glanced up into his taunting eyes and saw then that he was teasing her. It must be the drink, she thought, but was warmed by the fact that he caught her hand in his, and she felt that they must look like two lovers, the way he smooched over her as they went to the lounge.

The Parkes' house was not as grand as Portia House, but it was large, and standing in its own grounds appeared spaciously elegant. The afternoon had slipped away into early evening, and the wind which had died down considerably was cooler now as guests mingled and wandered in the garden.

'Do we have to stay, Joanna?' Adam asked with genuine regret.

'No, I suppose not, but it won't be for long, Adam. Roxanne will be disappointed if we don't put in an appearance at the disco, but we don't need to stay long. After all, that's mainly for their young friends.'

In the event the time passed rapidly. There were masses of presents to be admired, a constant serving of sandwiches, tea, coffee or alcoholic drinks, and at nine o'clock everyone returned to the Tullbury Arms Hotel where flashing lights and loud music could be heard streets away.

By now Joanna was feeling tired, but to please Roxanne and Martyn, who seemed to be a charming young man, she and Adam danced their way through a couple more hours before Adam finally said enough was enough. They said their goodbyes to the happy couple who were leaving for the airport and then they left themselves. Joanna expected Adam to drive straight to Willow-Weed Cottage, but she soon realised that he was making for Portia House.

'Adam, why?' she asked tiredly, as he pulled through the electrically operated gates.

'I live here, remember? And no way are you going back to the cottage on your own tonight.'

'But I haven't come prepared to stay overnight,' she insisted.

'I expect we can overcome any practical problems, Joanna.'

She only paid half her attention to the little warning voice which pounded in her weary brain. Adam wouldn't, couldn't be planning seduction as they were both just too tired. The dogs barked furiously until he quietened them, and while he put the car away and locked the house securely Joanna went into the lounge. Soft lights had come on automatically, and the room was bathed in a gentle pinkish glow which immediately calmed her as she settled in the luxury of the comfortable settee.

When Adam joined her he had already removed his jacket and tie.

'Phew!' he said. 'That's better.'

'Don't be so mean,' Joanna protested. 'It's been a lovely day. I've thoroughly enjoyed it.'

He sat beside her and slid his arm along the back of the settee.

'And there's more,' he quipped, mimicking the well-known Irish comedian. 'To have this time to ourselves, alone, darling, is too good an opportunity to miss. It's no good fighting me, Joanna. I know you want me as much as I want you.'

She started to remonstrate, but his mouth descended on hers in such a sensual way that any rebuttal was futile. Before she knew it he had pulled her down into his arms, his fingers running round the neck edge of her dress while he kissed her with hungry passion.

'No, Joanna,' he said, suddenly pushing her away. 'There's no need for this here—come on.' She allowed herself to be taken up the wide staircase and into his bedroom where he unzipped her dress, and as it slid to the floor he picked it up and placed it on a hanger in his wardrobe. He stood surveying her in the soft-hued light. The atmosphere was filled with emotion and exciting expectation. Joanna willed him to come to her and while she unbuttoned his shirt he loosened the clasp of her bra. He pulled her down on to the side of the bed and with a deftness of touch he undid the suspenders which had kept her stockings up. As he rolled them gently down over her legs his loving expression drew from her the response he wanted. Her slim graceful fingers caressed his lean hard chest, her thumb toyed over protruding nipples.

'How exciting to find a girl who wears suspenders and silk stockings. You can't imagine what the glimpse of those few inches of bare thigh did for me today. But next time choose black underwear. It's so provocative.'

'Adam, I didn't dress to be provocative.'

'No? Then you should have done. But it's the undressing

which is important.' He slid the straps of her bra off her
shoulders and tossed the brief garment over his shoulder.
Then his eyes focussed on her nakedness and with a gentle
touch he smoothed his finger tips over the scar which ran
down her side.

'My poor darling,' he crooned, as he kissed the wrinkled
tissue.

'I'm sorry,' she whispered on the verge of tears. 'I should
have told you.'

Adam leaned back and stared directly into her eyes. 'You
thought I didn't know? My dear Joanna, how naïve can you
be? It's all in your medical history, but it isn't the kind of
thing one discusses. I realised that you had a particular
reason for wanting to come to Ampfield, I knew from Julian
that you wanted it kept a secret.'

'You've known all this time?' she asked.

'Of course, but I couldn't betray a confidence and I knew
that when you were ready you'd talk about it.'

Tears spilled out from Joanna's burning eyes, but she was
unable to speak, and as he caressed and explored with an
intimacy which had nothing to do with her outer skin, her
inner soul reached out to grasp all that he offered. It might
not be love, for no man could love so scarred a human form,
but it was a sympathetic consummation which took her to
the heights of physical ecstasy, and afterwards she lay
passively in Adam's arms, grateful for his whispered words
of comfort which soothed her to sleep.

The jingle of cups and saucers woke her at well past nine
o'clock next morning. She felt so deliciously comfortable,
though somewhat awed to find that she was still naked. It
all seemed like a dream from which she must surely wake.
Adam stooped over her, his short dressing-gown in dark red
edged with black falling forward to reveal the mat of dark
satin hair which adorned his chest. Joanna longed to run
her fingers through it again, to recapture the magic of the
moments of blissful intimacy which she could hardly
believe had occurred.

'Come on, sleepyhead, tea up!'

Joanna raised her arms above her head, stretching provocatively, and in an instant Adam caught her up in a bear-like hug. He sat on the side of the bed, his arm around her as they sipped their tea, and then he slipped in bed beside her again to stimulate and bring alive her natural instincts to beg for his loving touch.

If only this were real love, she thought as she held him close, drawing his head towards her so that their lips consorted together to increase the powerful feelings which swept them along on the swirling tide of ever-increasing passion . . .

As the tide ebbed away and seemingly out of grasp for ever Joanna's guilt returned. She had accepted Adam's demonstrative physical attention in a selfish way because she loved him so fiercely, but that he was using her she had no doubt at all. She fought back impassioned tears in an effort to absolve her true feelings for him. It was imperative to hang on to the wonderful pinnacle to which he had taken her, yet she knew that coming down to earth would cause an anguish of mind she wasn't up to enduring. She lay still, listening intently to each expelling breath as he fought for self-control.

Adam groaned and rolled over to face her, his body still partially covering hers on the side where her scars were.

'You're really something,' he whispered. 'What's taken us so long?'

Joanna sighed and tweaked his ear. She had to destroy her feelings for him, and being facetious was the only way.

'You wanted my cottage,' she said, laughing at him. 'I suppose this is my reward—but thanks, you've paid your debt. I suppose once you reach a certain point feelings overtake outward appearances. I never intended that anyone should have to look at my body.'

Adam leaned back, not to look at her scars but to glare into her eyes angrily. 'My God, Joanna!' he exclaimed, 'you really are hell-bent on persecuting yourself. You aren't the only girl in the world with scars—the worst ones you've got are in your mind.'

'Not after all these years,' she replied. 'Believe me, you

have to work out your own salvation after going through the kind of hell-fire I went through. Even people like Dr O'Brien only understand and help up to a certain point, and then it's up to the individual. I don't need to look at myself to know how hideous my body is. But I don't intend to be a freak either, so people must take me as I am.'

'The only pity I have for you, my girl, is that you're so damned full of self-pity. We all love you for what *you* are, for your kind heart and your devotion to helping patients in similar circumstances to yourself. As far as I'm concerned I don't even think about what happened years ago. That's all in the past, it's your future that counts.'

'My future is my business, Adam.'

'You're one of my staff and I care about you.'

Joanna couldn't bear a continuation of the conversation. She slipped from underneath him, but before she could reach the door Adam was after her, and she found herself in his strong arms again. He kissed her savagely.

'Stop torturing yourself. To me you're every inch a woman—and that's all a man needs,' he growled playfully.

'Let me go, Adam. I intended to go to church this morning—it's Harvest Festival—and I need to go to the bathroom.'

He relaxed his hold but didn't release her completely.

'We'll go to church together. Only God could make the love between man and woman so unique, so unutterably desirable, and we'll make our own thanksgiving. You take the bathroom and soak away those silly notions which you love to harbour, and I'll have a shower. We'll have time for a cup of coffee and then after church we'll go back to your cottage for the rest of the day.'

'I'm sure you had other plans for today. Don't let me coerce you into going to church if you hadn't intended to.'

He turned her round and sent her off with a sharp smack on her bottom, and she heard the gravelly sound he made in his throat when he chuckled.

As she lay in the bath soaking away her intense feelings for Adam she knew that the hurt of loving him was not so easily dispelled. She didn't think she could go to church

where emotions would be brought to the fore again, but in
the event Adam was the one doing the coercing, and she
found new strength in being with him. The Cathedral was
full, the service inspiring, and then with Joanna sitting
beside him in his sports car they headed for Willow-Weed
Cottage, and as they turned into the drive Adam put his
foot on the brakes so hard that had she not been wearing her
seat-belt Joanna would have gone hurtling through the
windscreen. A large, shiny-new saloon car stood in her
driveway—the one they knew belonged to Das.

Joanna looked across at Adam, who was staring ahead
with lips compressed together in displeasure.

'Das must have brought Kamla back by car,' Joanna said
to break the akward silence.

'How very observant of you, Joanna.' Adam said crisply,
and slowly moved the car forward to come to rest beside the
larger one.

'Did you know they were coming back today?' she asked.

'Kamla had to return for work,' he said brusquely.

Joanna decided not to say anything more. She unstrapped
herself and got out, found her key from her bag and let
herself in with Adam close behind her. The lounge was
empty except for cups left on the low coffee table, so Joanna
went to the kitchen where she found Kamla, wearing a
flimsy sari, standing at the worktop preparing a meal with
Das, in a very short white towelling robe, close beside her.
A cosy scene of domesticity. It was almost one o'clock and
they looked as if they had only just got up.

'How was the wedding?' Kamla asked with a broad smile.

'Exhausting, like most weddings,' Adam said. 'So after
the disco I took Joanna back to Portia House with me as I
didn't fancy her being here by herself, but apparently you
returned last night?'

Kamla looked directly at Adam and then at Das with a
knowing smile.

'We got back late—very late. You were right, Adam, the
cottage is a much quieter and more suitable place to hold an
earnest discussion than the busy city of Bath, splendid
though it is.'

'And the result of this earnest discussion?' Adam asked poignantly.

Kamla beamed radiantly, apparently unaware of Adam's hurt.

'Oh, that I have been rather neglectful of my parents' wishes and that given the chance to talk things over calmly the situation was not as hopeless as I suspected.'

'I think we can come to an amicable solution,' Das said, going to Kamla and putting his arm around her waist.

'Good,' Adam said with a hint of sarcasm in his tone. 'Then I suggest, Joanna, that we leave these two and go to find some lunch elsewhere?'

Joanna was lost for words, momentarily stunned by the situation, and she found herself following Adam back out to the car.

'I know a nice little pub where we can get a decent meal at the bar,' he said.

Joanna strapped herself in beside him again, but when they reached the top of the hill overlooking the great plains she asked him to pull in on to the grass verge.

'What's the matter?' he asked, looking concerned.

'You've set me up, Adam,' she accused hotly. 'You used me and my cottage to get Kamla and Das together. You even agreed to go to Roxanne's wedding to get me out of the way, and the nice little party we had at Portia House was all arranged by you to give them the opportunity of—doing whatever they've been doing—in *my* house!'

Adam's strained brows relaxed into a grin. 'The same as we were doing, I suspect.'

'Kamla must go,' Joanna said forcefully, not the least bit amused. 'And don't you every try to con me again, Adam. It doesn't seem to have taken Kamla long to be persuaded by Das, so the whole thing has been a hoax of the worst possible kind. If they can use my cottage to cohabit they can jolly well use Portia House as easily. Only you're in the way, I suppose? Well, don't think that you're worming your way into Willow-Weed, because I want it back the way it was—exclusively mine!'

Adam turned in his seat to look directly at her. He was

obviously shocked at her suppositions and accusations, but he patiently tried to reason with her.

'Darling, you've got it all wrong. None of this was planned—I wouldn't do that to anyone, least of all you. Das persuaded Kamla to meet him in Bath believing that if she saw where he worked, and they were on neutral territory, they could discuss their situation and get things sorted out. I suspect that Das is as surprised as us to see Kamla's reaction.'

'I'm sorry if you were hoping that things wouldn't be so easily resolved, Adam. Kamla is a charming girl and we've got on very well together, but it's understandable that she'd fall for someone of her own culture.'

'Kamla isn't a teenager. She just wants to continue her work unhindered, and their families wouldn't agree to them marrying and Kamla continuing with her career. That's why she decided to come to England to study further, so that she has more qualifications when she returns to India. There's plenty of need in her home country, but there was a great deal of pressure from their respective families. We in the West can't begin to understand their customs and attitudes—not wholly. But as to me setting the whole thing up—for heaven's sake don't let your imagination run away with you. I made love to you because I wanted to. Not because I was trying to patronise you on account of your injuries, which aren't nearly as horrific as you imagine, and certainly not because I was aiding and abetting Kamla and Das.' Adam faced the road, started up the engine and shot off without another word.

Joanna felt miserable. They hardly spoke during lunch, but that didn't matter because there were holidaymakers revelling in a noisy manner so conversation was almost impossible, and Joanna wasn't hungry anyway. Afterwards Adam drove to the coast, despite Joanna's protestations, and he tried to talk her round, but she remained adamant that she had been used, and that Kamla must go.

When they returned to Willow-Weed Cottage Das had already left, and Kamla had prepared a meal which they all enjoyed, though there was an underlying tension which

Joanna refused to help lighten.

'I'm sorry if you feel in any way inconvenienced, Joanna,' Kamla said with genuine regret. 'I can understand that you feel I misled you, but not intentionally. Das and I had not met for many years. It was a strange situation—and I had not bargained for the fact that he has become quite Westernised in his attitudes too. Believe it or not, he came to Ampfield to talk to me to try to dampen any ideas I might have had about wanting to marry him just to please our parents. Instead we found a mutual respect first, which developed into wanting to be friends, and then we found we both agreed that our careers were the most important. Now we think that we can make a working marriage possible.'

'But supposing you want to have children?'

Kamla smiled as only she could, with a flash of gleaming white teeth, as she placed her arm round Joanna's shoulders.

'That is already open for discussion,' she said. 'Maybe my career will become less important as time passes, but I haven't too much time left if I want to have babies of my own.'

Joanna noticed that Adam was looking less than pleased, and she felt sorry for him. Had all his hopes been dashed this weekend? Had he been depending on their relationship failing so that he could make himself available for Kamla?

'I am very tired now after travelling, so I will say goodnight,' Kamla said.

'I too am very tired. Goodnight, Adam.' Joanna hated being distant with Adam. She couldn't bear to hurt him, or see him hurt, yet she felt helpless, like an outsider, so the best thing was to leave him alone with Kamla for a while.

She shut herself away in her bedroom and paced the floor. Ideally she would like to have gone to the hospital and worked throughout the night to assuage her discontent, but that was not possible, so she undressed, thinking how ridiculous she must have looked in such a dressy outfit going for a pub lunch, but her appearance had pleased Adam, and that was all that mattered. Not even in her wildest dreams had she imagined that a glimpse of frivolous underwear would have such an effect on him.

However he felt now, or whatever misgivings she might have, the truth was that he had made her extremely happy for twenty-four hours or so. They had been compatible in spite of her doubts that any man would be able to let himself go once he had seen her without her clothes on. She would always believe he pitied her, even though he insisted that she only pitied herself. Not one word of love, of course, and perhaps she should be grateful, because it would have raised her hopes falsely. But nothing could erase the deep obsessive love she felt for Adam and would continue to feel, however much pain it caused her. She supposed he would up and leave Ampfield Hospital now that Kamla was betrothed to Das. The thought was almost too awful to bear, but she must will herself to be brave just as she had been in the past. If ever she needed Julian it was now, and when she heard Adam's car leave the drive a few minutes later she was about to rush downstairs to the telephone when she heard it ringing.

'Shall I answer it?' Kamla called from the stairs.

'No, I'm coming.' Joanna pushed her arms through her dressing-gown sleeves and ran down to the hall.

'Hullo,' she said breathlessly.

'Where have you been?' a male voice demanded, and Joanna's heart sank to its lowest ebb. How she had longed to hear Julian's voice, but instead it was her brother Philip's.

'Oh, it's you, Phil,' she said glumly.

'Don't sound so delighted to hear your own flesh and blood!' he said drily. 'I often ring on a Sunday evening. Have you been working?'

'No, I had the weekend off and I've been to a wedding.'

'What, today?'

'No, silly, yesterday, and today I've spent with a colleague. Have you phoned before, then?'

'Yes, I tried last evening, but there was no reply.'

'Is something wrong?' Joanna asked.

'No—but since you've got your paying guest there and we haven't been able to visit we wondered whether you'd like

to come up to London for a weekend, or longer if you can.
Bring the aunts too—Mum and Dad are flying over for a
short stay.'

'Oh yes, Mum did say something on her last leter, but
she's often saying they're coming and then they go
somewhere else.'

'Have you got some holiday to come?' Phil asked.

'Yes—I haven't been off all summer. When are they
coming?'

'Later this week. You know them—everything has to be
done on the spur of the moment, so you'd better make it
next weekend or you'll miss them.'

'Oh dear. I've just had a weekend—still, I am due some
holiday, but it's a bit short notice. I'll see what I can
arrange, Phil, and let you know.'

'There's no need. Just chivvy the old aunts along and
book in at the Cedar Grove Hotel like you did before. Sorry
we haven't got room for everyone here, but you know how
it is.'

Yes, Joanna did know just what the chaos would be like,
but it couldn't have been better timed. It would be good to
see her parents again even if they weren't actually coming
over from America to see her. It would be some necessary
business of her father's and their time together would be
short and sweet, but seeing Phil and his family would be a
happy diversion from events here at Ampfield.

'I'll see what I can arrange,' she agreed, and they ended
their conversation with general news. They weren't that
close, but Phil was always there if she needed help, and she
knew that he was glad she had Julian to depend on. But not
any more, she thought disconsolately as she wearily climbed
the stairs. He had Lynn now, and she must exercise this
independence she was so proud of.

The next day she saw the Senior Nursing Officer to make
arrangements to take a week's holiday.

'It's a bit short notice, Joanna,' the older woman said,
pursing her lips as she studied duty rostas.

'My parents are coming over from the States on a brief

visit,' Joanna explained. 'I'm sorry—and it doesn't matter, if it's putting anyone out.'

The SNO looked up sharply. 'Of course it matters. You hardly ever see them, so you must take some time off.' She looked up at Joanna with a warm smile. 'If only all the staff were so easy to handle, Joanna, my job would be much easier. You make so few demands of us, but I'm afraid we expect a great deal from you. It's time you had a holiday. I . . . um . . . er . . . it's nothing to do with me, I know, but it is my job to observe the staff and their comings and goings, and I notice that Julian and Lynn have become,' she raised her eyebrows questioningly, 'more than just good friends? I know you two have always been close, but maybe there was not so great a love?'

Joanna laughed. 'As you know, I knew Julian before I came to Ampfield, so if there had been a great love we'd have got married by now, I should think.'

'All the same, changing friendships can cause distress, you know, but I think you're pleased for Lynn?'

Joanna agreed that she was, and went back to duty grateful that the opportunity to get away for a short break was arranged.

Apart from the staff on her floor, Lynn and Julian, she told no one else until the day before she left, and then she gave the news to Kamla. Joanna had been too busy to think too much about the Indian doctor's situation. It was her life, hers and Das's, and they must do as they pleased. Whether Adam had used her as she suspected Joanna couldn't be certain, but she had plunged back into the spirit of her job to try and forget. The Malvin family had been discharged except for Elizabeth, who still needed treatment, and Matthew went home eager to be with his kitten, while Mr King was transferred to a nursing home to convalesce before he went home because the beds at Ampfield were so desperately needed. Joanna felt she was deserting a sinking ship, but for once she was utterly selfish in putting herself first, and as she sat beside her aunts in the taxi taking them to the station she experienced a feeling of relief at putting distance between herself and the dour expression on

Adam's face which he'd been wearing for the past week.

Once on the train, though, the miles slipped away beneath the wheels carrying her farther away from him, and she knew that part of her heart was trailing behind in the wake of a love which was tearing her apart.

CHAPTER TEN

AS ALWAYS the London station was jam-packed with people of all nationalities and age groups, and while Joanna's two aunts stayed with the luggage Joanna went to see if Phil was anywhere to be seen. He wasn't, so she returned to her aunts and took them to the buffet for a much-needed cup of tea.

'Phil said to wait here if he didn't show up on time,' she said. 'You keep my seat at this table and I'll fetch the tea. Did you want anything to eat?'

'No, my dear,' Aunt Marion said. 'Knowing Sheila, we shall have to struggle through a man-sized meal later on—and they always eat so late—it isn't good for my digestion.'

'Oh, go on with you, Marion,' Aunt Peg scorned. 'You know you never leave anything on your plate and the food is always delicious—but you're right, we'd better starve ourselves for the next hour or so. Can you manage, Joanna?'

'Yes, but there's a long queue, so you'll have to be patient. Watch out for Phil while I'm gone.'

Joanna went to join the long line of people armed with plastic trays, who were moving up slowly as they surveyed the contents of the glass cabinets for appetising snacks. She began to feel annoyed at having to trail monotonously behind when all she wanted was a pot of tea for three. She hated crowds, and she began to think nostalgically of Ampfield and her friends—Adam in particular. He hadn't really held a decent conversation with her during the past week, so she didn't know whether he was aware of her holiday or not. But what did it matter to him? Joanna felt certain that he was too put out by Kamla's sudden change of heart to even give her a second thought. Suddenly she felt a tug at her elbow and she looked round quickly expecting

151

to see her brother—instead it was a face from the past, a very disfigured but dear face.

'Carl!' she exclaimed with a sharp intake of breath. 'You, of all people—what are you doing here?'

'Up front getting tea—is that all you require?'

'Yes,' Joanna said, 'for three, my aunts are with me.'

'I know, I spotted them first. Go back to them at your table and I'll bring your tea.'

Joanna felt a bit guilty about putting her tray back in the rack, but as Carl was already being served it would save time in the long run. She wound her way through the busy cafeteria to where she had left her aunts.

'That was a spot of luck, dear,' Aunt Marion said. 'Fancy Carl remembering us!'

'Isn't it nice of him, he's getting our pot of tea.'

'Poor boy,' Aunt Marion said sympathetically. 'Life can't have been easy for him with a face like that.'

'It isn't nearly as bad as I recall from when the accident occurred. The scars do fade, don't they, Joanna?' Aunt Peg said.

'Yes, all scarred tissue repairs to a certain degree, but he's had loads of skin grafts, by the looks of things. It tends to change one's appearance, but he looks remarkably well, though older, of course, like me.'

'You've matured, my dear,' Aunt Marion said. 'You've—blossomed as the years have passed—and more so recently.'

Joanna made a face at her aunt, adding a warning signal too as Carl had reached their table with a laden tray.

'That was a bit sneaky,' Joanna laughed. 'But thanks very much. Are you alone——?' She gazed round, expecting that perhaps he was with someone at another table.'

'Quite alone, Joanna. Gosh, it is good to see you, and you're looking so well. I've just come back from Scandinavia.'

'Mm, interesting. What have you been doing in Scandinavia?'

'Selling sausage skins—and with a face like mine who better to get sympathy?' Carl laughed heartily.

'Oh, Carl, don't say things like that. Were you pulling my leg? You can't really sell sausage skins, can you?'

'Among other things required in the retail trade, yes—for my father's firm. But tell me how the world has been treating you?'

Joanna wanted to cry on his shoulder and say 'cruelly', but that would be giving way to more of that self-pity Adam had accused her of having, so she smiled congenially and told him where she worked.

'Mum and Dad are home from the States, so I had to make a fast decision to come to Phil's to see them. Have you seen Phil lately?'

'Not for about two years, but then I travel abroad quite a bit now. At first when all the grafts were completed and I'd regained some confidence I accompanied the senior rep. He was a real character, full of fun, always ready to put himself down and everyone else. He was just what I needed to get me out among people, and as I was the boss's son his customers felt sorry for me, so business boomed as a result.'

'Now you travel around alone, then?' Joanna asked.

'Yes.' Carl's face clouded for a moment. 'Poor old Pete, ate too much, drank too much, indulged in every way, which finally resulted in a massive heart attack when we were in Austria. We did everything we could for him, but he didn't stand a chance and died within a matter of hours. I contacted my father, who simply told me to get on and do whatever had to be done, so I did, and gradually earned the customers' respect, and I just love travelling all over the world—and all to sell sausage skins, which as one customer said I could well do with to cover my own face.'

'How cruel!' Aunt Peg said in disgust.

'No, Miss Morris, not really. When you find out that you're a bit of a freak you have to join in and laugh at yourself. It's the only way.' Carl turned and looked at Joanna. 'You were lucky, Joanna. Your scars can be hidden from view.'

She returned his intense gaze, knowing that they were both remembering that ghastly night. 'Yes, I was lucky,

Carl,' she agreed, 'though there are some scars which will
never heal. I think so often about little Emma and how
heartbroken her grandparents were.'

Suddenly Aunt Peg waved frantically to someone across
the room and Joanna saw her brother looking for them. He
strode across the floor in an authoratitive way when Aunt
Peg caught his eye, and his expression visibly lifted when
he saw who was with them.

'Well, if it isn't old sausage skin himself!' he said jovially.
'Don't tell me you just happened to bump into the
family—or have you and Joanna been cooking something up
between you without us knowing?'

'If I'd known where to find her I might have done,' Carl
confessed. 'And you might not believe this, but I seldom
stop here for anything, I prefer to get home.'

'Married yet?' Phil asked.

'You've got to be joking—who'd want me? I'm lucky,
though, to have caring parents.'

'Ours are just in from the States. Look,' Phil said eagerly,
'we must all get together. Give me your phone number and
I'll get in touch to make arrangements.'

'That's a great idea, but if they're not here for long you'll
want to be just the family.'

'Nonsense,' Phil insisted, 'they'd love to see you and your
folks, so we'll have a dinner party. That'd be nice, wouldn't
it, Joanna?'

'Yes, but you'd better check with Sheila first.'

'She'll be thrilled to see you again, Carl.'

'And I shall look forward to seeing her. You were both
pretty good to me when I was first in the London hospital.
That's when you realise who your friends are, isn't it,
Joanna?' Carl touched Phil's arm. 'I was saying, your
sister looks pretty good to me. It's been a long time—too
long.'

A glance at Aunt Marion warned Joanna that implications
were already under way. She and Carl had enjoyed many
happy hours together during their teenage years, but now
time and events had taken them along separate paths, and
Joanna was sensible enough to realise that they were both

very different people from nine years ago. She hoped no one
was going to read too much into this casual meeting. It was
good to see him again, though, she was saddened to be
reminded of the awful incident which had resulted in Carl
almost losing an eye, and most of his hair, though that had
grown again and was even better than previously. She
didn't know about the rest of his body, except that at the
time he had received extensive burns which had kept him in
hospital for the best part of two years. There had been times
of remission when he had gone home to rest and to give the
skin grafts time to heal completely before further work
was done, just as in her own case. She was lucky. Outwardly
she bore no scars, but Carl couldn't hide his
facial disfigurement and Joanna was consumed with
pity.

They all wandered out to Phil's car, which was parked
close by on a parking meter, and Carl said goodbye as he
hailed a taxi.

'Afraid he goes in the opposite direction to us and there
isn't room for five comfortably when there's luggage as
well,' Phil said. 'In any case, he's going to his office first,
and that's only minutes away in the city.'

'He looks well,' Joanna said. 'Poor Carl, he came off quite
badly, though, didn't he?'

'Well, don't tell him that,' Phil said sharply. 'He hates to
be pitied and he's given up worrying too much about his
appearance, he prefers to make light of it.'

'I realise that,' Joanna said. 'But if it hadn't been for me
and Emma he could easily have got out of the fire
unscathed.'

'Apportioning blame is a useless exercise too, Joanna. I
thought you'd got over all that.'

'I have, but seeing Carl again brings back memories.'

'Maybe it's a good thing you have met up again . . .' Aunt
Marion began.

'No, no matchmaking, please!' Joanna begged
lightheartedly.

'I wasn't suggesting anything,' Aunt Marion insisted
indignantly. 'What I meant was that you can see for

yourself how he's coped with life, and is apparently enjoying himself. He always was a nice young man and you were such good friends.'

'I hope we still are, but naturally living so far apart we lost touch. Maybe he's got a girlfriend?' Joanna was sitting beside her brother in the car as he drove precariously through London's busy traffic. She glanced across at him as she spoke.

'Not any more,' Phil said. 'He was engaged to be married, to a nurse he met while he was in hospital, but she went off with a doctor, like most of them do.'

'Not most,' Joanna quipped. 'There aren't enough to go round, and they aren't all the marrying kind.'

'You've had a good run for your money with Julian,' Aunt Peg said. 'I can't think why you didn't get married long ago. Now you've let this Lynn girl take him away.'

Joanna laughed and peered into her brother's face. 'They don't change, do they?'

Phil laughed too, then he said quite seriously: 'Why didn't you marry Julian, Joanna? You and he seemed so right for each other—we all thought it was a foregone conclusion.'

'Then you were wrong,' she answered positively. 'If we'd rushed into marriage it would probably have been a disaster. I would never have been sure that it wasn't because everyone expected it, or that Julian just felt sorry for me. Working together finally sorted our emotions out—and I know I didn't feel deeply enough for him to marry him. Lynn is exactly right and they're very happy.'

'And there's no one else?' Phil asked with concern.

'No one.' Joanna's voice cracked a little, giving her away, but the occupants of the car fell silent and after a twenty-minute drive they pulled up outside a smart house not far from Hatton Garden.

Reunions were happy but tearful, and after supper Phil drove Joanna and the two aunts to the nearby hotel where they usually stayed. Joanna was grateful for the privacy of her single room, where she stood out on the small iron balcony and watched London's night life go by for a while before she prepared for bed.

Sleep didn't come easily, not only because of the unfamiliar sounds but because her thoughts flew back to Ampfield and Adam. She wished she had found the courage to go to him and confront him with her regrets that Kamla and Das had fallen in love, which meant that he was out of the running. Because she loved him so desperately she shared his disappointment, and his anguish of a lost love mingled with her own. At least she had talked with Julian and Lynn before she left, explaining about the situation at Willow-Weed Cottage. She didn't think they believed she was visiting her brother to see her parents, as they openly accused her of running away, but for once she wasn't, though she was thankful that fate had intervened the way it had. Was it fate too which had taken Carl into the buffet at the same time that she was there? She wished she could say it had thrilled her beyond measure to see him again, but, while she was immensely pleased, in her heart the ache of loving Adam was like an open wound gnawing and burrowing into her very soul.

It was strange to be part of the family again, and after breakfast each day Joanna and her aunts walked the short distance to Phil's home where they could relax, and Joanna and her parents were able to catch up on all the latest news. Within a few hours Joanna felt that she was being drawn closer to them. They showed more concern for her than she had ever been aware of before. Was it because as they grew older they were realising just how much of their children they were missing? Joanna and Phil had proved that they could survive without them, but now Joanna felt as if the tables were turned, that her mother was needing her. She perceived that they were both looking older. Her mother was still a slim, elegant woman, fashionably dressed to complement her distinguished-looking husband, who had a charming manner and a computer-like brain where his job was concerned, but in spite of the pleasantries and go-ahead attitude Joanna suspected that they were beginning to run down. Her mother joked about growing old gracefully, while her father seemed to be practising speeches about bowing out to make way for a younger man, and Phil frequently caught Joanna's eye with a meaningful look.

It was at the dinner party when Carl brought his parents along for a grand reunion that Mr Morris dropped his bombshell.

'I'm retiring from the Foreign Office,' he said after dinner. 'I've got a nice little business number lined up, but I could do with some help and I want my children to share in our good fortune—a fortune which could benefit all of us, so what say you kids pack up here in old England and come out to join us? We're getting on now and we look forward to having more time to spend with you and our grandchildren—if we're lucky, that is. Joanna, you seem to be stuck in a rut in that profession of yours, and Phil, you could earn far more in the States than here.'

Phil raised his hand. 'Hold on, Dad!' he said. 'You've never suggested such a thing before, and you're travelled all over the place with the Foreign Office. Evidently you've found a niche in America, and Joanna and I are pleased about that, but you can't expect us to cut ourselves off from our friends and jobs just like that.'

Joanna sensed a bristling of everyone's nerves. Her parents had spent many years travelling and living abroad. No mention had ever been made of including their children—in fact Joanna sometimes wondered whether they remembered they had any—and now suddenly she and Phil had become important to them. Could it be that they felt guilty at never including them in their lives, or were they beginning to realise that there would be no one of their own to look after them in their old age? Just how selfish could people be?

'And why can't you come back to where you belong to spend your last days, might I ask?' Aunt Peg said with a critical sniff.

'Last days?' Mrs Morris echoed. 'My dear Marion, I hope we aren't done for yet, just because John has finished with the Foreign Office.'

'Joanna and Philip have had to fend for themselves all these years, so why would they want to up and change their lifestyle now, just when it suits you?' Aunt Marion demanded.

Joanna almost felt sorry for her father, who had evidently thought he was making some grand gesture. He drew on his fat cigar, sending foul-smelling smoke around the dining room to add insult to injury.

'Speaking for myself,' Joanna said as calmly as she could, 'I don't feel as if I'm in a rut. I do a job I love, I have plenty of friends and dear Aunt Peg and Aunt Marion to go to when I need a change, or when they need me, and Phil and Sheila here, so I can't think of one good reason why I should contemplate uprooting myself at present.'

'Perhaps not just yet,' her father said with a hint of hurt in his tone, 'but aren't your parents a good enough reason for changing the habits of a lifetime?'

'No, Dad,' Phil said emphatically. 'I'm doing very well here in London, and Sheila likes being near to her family. I couldn't possibly uproot everything now—besides, we're hoping to start a family soon and Sheila naturally wants to be near her parents.'

'Oh well,' Mr Morris said, waving his cigar in the air, 'it was just a thought. I have business interests which need a good reliable accountant and I thought who better to offer the job to than my own son, but if you don't want it there's plenty who'll jump at the chance.'

Carl very cleverly changed the direction of the conversation to business generally all over the world, and in particular the amusing side of selling sausage skins, much to everyone's relief, but a strained atmosphere still lingered and Joanna was thankful when Carl's parents decided to make a move.

'I'll come on later,' Carl told them. 'I'm going to see Joanna and her aunts back to the hotel.'

They were glad of the fresh air, and some indignant exchanges took place between the aunts.

'They've never bothered about the children until now.

Phil and Joanna have been like ours,' Aunt Peg grumbled.
'And now they're giving no thought to our welfare.'

'Thoroughly selfish,' Aunt Marion accused. 'If it hadn't
been for Carl and his parents being there I could have said a
great deal on the subject of family life!'

Carl took Joanna's hand in his and squeezed, and she felt
a quiver of amusement transfer from him to her. When they
reached the hotel he offered them a drink in the bar, but the
aunts were too upset and tired, so Joanna saw them up to
their room and then returned to the bar downstairs where
Carl was waiting.

'Poor darlings,' Joanna sympathised. 'Dad is so
undiplomatic for a Foreign Office diplomat, and what a
cheek, suggesting that I'm in a rut!'

'Well, aren't you?' Carl grinned. 'Joanna, it's been the
hell of a long time—too damned long. Can we——?' he
shrugged, 'at least make up for lost time?'

Joanna smiled and accepted the drink he had ordered for
her. 'You're right, Carl, it's been too long, but seeing you
again has been a bonus I hadn't bargained for—sausage
skins and all!' They laughed together happily just as if the
years rolled away and they were teenagers again. It wasn't
until Carl kissed her goodnight and Joanna felt the uneven
skin of the grafts on his cheeks that she was reminded about
his injuries. All these years she had worried about her
appearance when no one ever saw any sign of her suffering,
while Carl had to face the world with a disfigurement which
wasn't exactly ugly but was certainly unsightly.

'Let's have dinner together while you're here, Joey?' Carl
said softly.

'That would be nice. I don't suppose the parents will stay
long now. I can't imagine what's happened to make them
feel guilty about Phil and me all of a sudden, but I'm afraid
they'll have to go away empty-handed. We've grown up,
which is something they hadn't accounted for. I suspect
there's more to it than just wanting us around. As I'm a
nurse maybe they see me in the role of nursemaid to them
in their old age, and Phil being a whizz-kid with money,
Dad has earmarked him to make him a millionaire. It's

pathetic, Carl, don't you think, to try to use people like that?'

'We all have to use one another in various ways, but I agree your father's attitude does seem to be selfishly mercenary. In every other way it was a good dinner party. How about tomorrow? I'll pick you up at eight —OK?'

Joanna agreed and went to bed in happy anticipation, though uneasy about her parents. She began to fancy that one of them might be ill, but her aunts soon talked her out of that idea next morning at breakfast, and when they reached Phil's house suitcases and bags were already standing in the hall.

They went as a family to Heathrow to see them off, and Joanna felt sad, wishing that things might have been different.

'They'll never change, Joanna,' Phil said half-apologetically. 'That's what position and money does for you. They don't have any deep feelings for us—we're almost strangers, and if it's any consolation to you, all that rubbish about wanting us to go out there is because someone has ripped Dad off to the tune of a few thousand dollars and he's peeved. To make matters worse it's apparently the son of one of Mum's best friends at her bridge club, so they were feeling rather sorry for themselves. They'll get over it, and I've promised that we'll try to take a trip over there one day.' He pulled Joanna sharply up against his side and squeezed her with brotherly protection. 'But I didn't say which day!'

'Or year!' Joanna countered.

'As long as we stick together that's all that matters, and we do have the loyal aunts to care for, they've been so good to us. I am worried about you, though. I wish—well, that there was someone in your life—someone special.'

'Mm . . .' Joanna hedged uncertainly. It was a great temptation to spill the beans to her brother, but somehow she couldn't bring herself to speak of Adam and her love for him just at this moment. 'I'm only twenty-five, Phil. There's plenty of time—isn't there?'

'Of course—he'll be worth waiting for when he does show up.'

'By the way, I'm eating out tonight. With Carl—and before you say anything, no, there isn't anything going on—it's just for old times' sake.'

'Good, he's nice, and he'll look after you. I suppose in a way you're both in the same boat, having suffered similar injuries.'

'Carl's were much worse than mine, but he's good fun, he makes me laugh, and with us we don't have to pretend, so we can have a nice easy friendship—but I do mean friendship, Phil. Don't go getting ideas, and don't let the aunts get any either. You know what they are. Aunt Marion will have the sewing machine out!'

'You go out and have a good time while you've got the chance. I'm only sorry that we haven't been able to get down to stay with you, but Sheila's been busy now that she's in charge of her department. She's got this idea in her head that she must have everything in order before we start trying seriously for a baby, so apart from the week we had in Portugal with friends we haven't had any holiday. She's already anticipating morning sickness.'

'Send her down to me if she suffers from that. You know I'd love to have you now that the cottage is mine, but I don't think the Indian doctor will be with me for very much longer, so try to have a break before the winter, Phil.'

'Will do, but you ought to get away yourself.'

'I'm here now, aren't I?'

'Go somewhere hot and exciting, Joanna. Can't you get Carl to take you with him on one of his trips?'

'That sounds like a good idea, but I'm not sure that I'd want to. Let's see how the dinner date goes first.'

It surpassed all Joanna's expectations. They ate at one of London's finest restaurants where sometimes celebrities could be seen, and after that Carl took Joanna to a night club where they danced the midnight hour away, drank too much good wine and entered into the spirit of the rather dubious cabaret act.

'Not quite a strip-tease, but nearly,' Joanna said.

'Something we couldn't do anyway,' Carl responded, laughing, and when the time came for them to depart he held her in his arms and kissed her tenderly as they cuddled in the back seat of the taxi. 'You can't know what this has done for my ego, Joanna darling.'

His kisses lacked the fire which Adam had kindled, and although Joanna did her best to enjoy Carl's attention the magic was not present. 'You could stay with me tonight,' he whispered. 'It would please me so much.'

Joanna drew away and looked up into his face. 'Carl, let's not rush things. Besides, can you imagine the aunts' faces if they went to look for me in my room and I wasn't there?'

'You might be out for an early constitutional?' Carl suggested, and because Joanna suspected an element of relief they laughed the tension away before saying a prolonged goodnight.

The week passed by so quickly that Joanna was on her way back to Ampfield before she knew it. The train journey was tedious from London to her aunts' home, and then after spending a night with them she returned to Willow-Weed Cottage by car just as she had travelled on the outward journey. It had been pleasant, yes, very pleasant, she decided, and the more so because she had met Carl again. In spite of all her resolutions not to let him inveigle his way into her affections they had grown warm and contented in each other's company. But she'd known him for most of her life, she argued, he was more like a brother—well, perhaps not quite, there had been some dangerously intimate moments before she had left—but she had to admit that they were comfortable in each other's company. She hadn't been prepared for a marriage proposal, though, and the worst of that was that she didn't want to hurt Carl.

She stroked her chin thoughtfully as she let the car cruise through the country lanes outside Tullbury. Would it work? Could she make Carl happy? God knows he deserved it after all that he'd been through, and she did blame herself partly for his injuries. If it hadn't been for her he would have concentrated on getting himself out of the dance hall pronto. But did she really owe him enough to commit herself to spending the rest of her life with him? It could never be love, she thought dismally. Yes, it might, she contradicted, love might grow from their mutual respect for one another. But there would always be Adam. However hard she tried to dismiss him he would haunt her—those precious words of comfort he had whispered at the height of their ecstasy; no one could ever compete with Adam's impetuous stimulation. Just the thought of it stirred her very nerve-ends to desire, and she nearly ran off on to the verge. Pull yourself together, she told herself angrily. There was no point in letting imagination run away with her. Adam didn't want her, he had only used her, and look where that had got him. He's lost Kamla—*but*, she thought, not quite. Kamla and Das weren't married yet, and there was still plenty of time for Adam to concoct some other plan to thwart his rival. As long as he didn't involve her, though . . .

Suddenly a car came towards her at a mad speed on such a narrow road. Joanna had the presence of mind to steer into the grass verge where luckily an open farm gate prevented her from crashing. Her head spun. The other car—it was Adam's, and as she sat still regaining her breath there was a loud revving as his car reversed alongside hers. He got out, slamming the door furiously.

'Why don't you look where you're going?' he shouted in at the window which was only open a crack. 'Joanna!'

'Who else drives an old white beetle round here?' she retorted.

'I wasn't concentrating . . .' he began, then stopped short, realising how he had incriminated himself.

'That was fairly obvious,' she said, winding down the window. Just the sight of his face, even though it was grooved with anger, made her heart flip over.

'So you've decided to return?' he said sarcastically. 'You

didn't say that you were going away on holiday this month. It was a shock when Kamla told me you'd already gone.'

'I don't have to account to you, do I? It's true the arrangements were made in rather a hurry, because my parents have been home from the States. The SNO understands my position. After more than three years she's used to me having to make rushed arrangements for holiday, but I daresay you've never noticed, and wouldn't now if it hadn't been for Kamla. I suppose it was all right for her to stay alone at Willow-Weed Cottage?'

Adam almost ground his teeth at her. 'You can be so childish at times, Joanna. I'm as concerned over Kamla being at the cottage alone as I am over you. It's so isolated, and now that the evenings are drawing in it can't be the ideal place to be alone.'

'I've always quite liked it. In fact, as I've said before, I prefer to live alone.'

'Humph!' Adam snorted angrily. 'You're going to have your eyes opened dramatically when you get married, *and* as I recall, you aren't averse to male company when it suits you.'

Joanna's cheeks burned uncomfortably. 'That's not fair!' she said hotly. 'Since you were the male involved you know only too well that your little scheme was all arranged to allow Kamla and Das time to have my cottage to themselves. Whatever the wrongs and rights of their culture, it hasn't taken them long to learn our low standards.'

'Careful, Joanna—you didn't give me the impression of resisting my attention, which had nothing to do with low standards.'

'No!' she argued defiantly. 'Pure and simple selfishness.' She switched the engine on again and the loud chug of her noisy engine made further conversation impossible.

'Time you got rid of this antiquated heap of junk.'

It was Joanna's turn to grind her teeth as she changed gear and let out the clutch, hating him for his sudden grin, especially as she might almost have construed an element of affection in his expression.

'You just mark my words,' he said dominantly. 'This thing is going to let you down one dark night and you'll be easy prey for some rapist on the prowl. Remind me to get you a bleeper—at least I shall feel happier.'

'Don't bother,' Joanna said. 'If you'll excuse me, I'm anxious to get home.'

Adam stood aside to allow her to reverse out on to the road again. Bleeper indeed! she thought aggressively. But by the time she reached Willow-Weed she was wearing quite a sensuous smile. Just the fact of a brief meeting with him had been enough to make her glad to be back.

CHAPTER ELEVEN

SUMMER was over, and blustery autumn winds swept across the countryside bringing a winter chill necessitating putting the heating on, and searching out light woollen clothes. The wards were full and operating theatres kept busy with skin grafts of varying degrees as well as other cosmetic surgery. A young farmer was brought in with his arm hanging off, the result of a chain-saw accident, but with speed and expertise Adam was able to stitch the arm back in place, and after the effects of shock had subsided Kenny Leighton was transferred to the main ward.

Joanna, being short of staff owing to a bout of 'flu in the hospital, did the round of checking pulses and temperatures.

'How do you feel today, Kenny?' she asked as she fluffed up his pillows and tidied his bed.

'Bit shaky still, but I'm OK. Can't believe I've still got me arm, Sister.'

'Quick action is what's necessary in cases like yours. I guess you won't be in such a hurry to use a chain-saw again.'

'All part of me job—and at least it looks as if I'll still be able to work on the farm, though Mr Royston says the arm will never be quite the same again. Still,' he added with a grin, 'it's what me right arm's for that really counts, and I'll manage to get a glass to me lips, however awkward.'

Joanna laughed as she went to the next patient. The area was rural with acres of arable land so that accidents from the misuse of farming implements were all too frequent, though they prided themselves on a high rate of success, and Kenny was going to be one of them, she felt sure.

Kamla had greeted Joanna back warmly, and Joanna

accepted the situation as unchanged. Kamla was in Ampfield for a year's work, so she might as well remain at Willow-Weed Cottage for that time. Das was an occasional visitor at weekends and sometimes Kamla went to Bath, but Joanna refrained from asking what their arrangements were. Her own social life was becoming quite hectic, as Carl turned up unexpectedly one weekend and when he couldn't find Milton Lane and Joanna's cottage he arrived at the hospital. He was quite used to finding accommodation for himself and booked himself in at the Ploughman's Furrow Inn before Joanna took him to the hospital canteen.

'You should have let me know you were coming,' she said as all eyes vetted the stocky, broad-shouldered man by her side.

'Then you'd have put me off, Joey. It's a good job I'm thoroughly familiar with hospitals, as I feel a bit like a monkey in a cage with all these pretty nurses staring at me.'

Joanna bought the coffee and sandwiches and led the way to a corner table in a crowded canteen.

'Anyone strange invokes interest.'

'I'll accede to the "strange", but I did think here of all places they'd be used to freaks like me without needing to stare.'

'Don't kid yourself it's on account of your facial scars, Carl,' she said firmly. 'You're a man, obviously a friend of mine whom no one has seen or heard of before, so naturally there's got to be speculation.'

'I hope there's good reason for that, Joanna,' he said, gazing earnestly into her face. 'That's why I've come. You didn't reject me out of hand—maybe I read the signs wrongly, but I believed there might be reason to follow up my proposal. I've been in Europe since we met in London, so I can take a week or so off now and I thought I'd come down this way to see where you hang out.'

'It's nice to see you again, Carl. The years have gone by so fast, those village dances a thing of the past, and we mustn't get carried away. We aren't quite the same people, you know.'

'No, indeed not. We're older, wiser, each understanding the other's problems, I believe, so we could make an ideal marriage. You know I always cared for you a great deal, but we were only kids then. Maybe if it hadn't been for the accident we'd have gone on seeing each other at holiday times and would have been married ages ago.'

Joanna laughed this off. 'I very much doubt that, Carl,' she said. 'You were going to join the Navy and travel the world by kind permission of Her Majesty's government—remember?'

'How could I forget? My fate might have been exactly the same, Joanna. I might have been in the Falklands war. Every time I see the effects of fire aboard ships I'm reminded of how I look. You might even have been a war widow!'

'For goodness' sake, Carl, don't be so morbid!'

His seriousness didn't last more than a moment or two, and then she saw the twinkle back in his eye. He couldn't hide the mischief which was always just beneath the surface, ready to explode at a second's notice. That was one thing Joanna was glad about, that he hadn't become bitter and twisted in spite of all that had happened.

'And what about your dreams?' he reminded her gently. 'A business tycoon, wasn't it? Had to be someone with at least two holiday homes, one in Monaco and the other in Switzerland, and two of everything else? You didn't mean to have to work for your living. Most of all you wanted a nice home, and a husband who was content to live what you called an honest civilian life, happy to stay at home with his wife and family, and be everything to you your father was not. I guess you were looking for a father figure—did you never find him, Joanna?'

'Hm,' she mused, 'the Godfather!'

'The what?'

'Oh, nothing. Yes, Carl, I reckon I did find what I was looking for, but *I* wasn't quite what he wanted. He needed a tool, someone to help him get what he wanted, but things didn't turn out quite right.'

'Does that mean that you'll never marry anyone else?'

'I . . . I honestly don't know—and this canteen is hardly the place for such serious conversation.'

'Then I can stay at Ampfield and we'll talk some more?'

Joanna shrugged. 'No harm in that, I suppose.'

They strolled back though the corridors to the main entrance, making arrangements for Carl to meet Joanna when she went off duty later.

'It's supposed to be seven o'clock, but in this job you never know,' she said.

Carl held her gently by the elbows. He was a gentle giant, she thought, and he should be doing something better than selling sausage skins.

'You look enchanting in that uniform, Joey. You've made good, you've even got something out of being in that fire, though surely through your patients you relive that nightmare every day almost?'

'No, Carl. It's taken a long, long time, but I've just realised that I'm lucky to be alive, lucky to have a good job where I can help others and understand them better because of my experience. You ought to have trained in something similar.'

'A doctor? Male nurse? Me?'

'Why not? You had a good education and there are plenty of jobs in administration. Even social work, Carl. You'd be so good at that because you've got a good sense of humour.'

'But you wouldn't marry a sausage skin seller?'

'Don't be silly, I didn't mean that.'

'No, I know you didn't, but you think I'm wasting my time and talents? Joanna, my dear, we aren't all made the same way, and the kind of incident we were involved in has changed our lives dramatically by force of circumstance. Patients would look at me and imagine that they were going to look ten times worse. No, it was very fortunate for me that my parents owned a business and were willing to take me into it, scars and all. I've had to break down barriers through the years I've been with the company, but people

eventually accepted me, and commercially it's doing so well
that I could probably retire a millionaire at fifty—so there
you are, can you wait for another twenty years for your
millionaire, or shall we take a chance on what we've
got?'

'Money doesn't mean anything, Carl.' A car drew into
the car-park and when Joanna saw that it was Adam she
broke away from Carl's hold. 'I really must get back to
my floor, I've had far too long as it is. See you
later.'

It was just as if she had cut the tape across a new road.
Guilt flooded through like a sluice being open as she
realised that she was letting Carl think there was a chance
for him. One glance at Adam and she knew she couldn't be
unfaithful to him, even if his loyalty to her meant nothing.
She couldn't face him now, so she turned and hurried up
the stairs two at a time, reaching her office breathlessly.
From the window she motioned to Mary, her staff nurse,
that she was back and then she sat down to study the duty
roster and continue with some paperwork. It was after tea
when Adam came looking for her, and he came straight to
the point.

'Who was that you were seeing off after lunch today? I
didn't recognise him, though surely I should have done.
Did I do his grafts? Nice job, whoever did them, but surely
I'd remember. Must be an old patient?'

'No, Adam,' Joanna said calmly. 'He's never been a
patient here at Ampfield. Carl and I are old friends, we
were at that dance together and he tried to help me escape
the burning inferno. In consequence he was much more
badly injured than me. We happened to bump into each
other in London, so he thought he'd come down for a few
days.'

She felt her face reddening as Adam glared down at her.
Her throat had gone dry, her voice husky as she'd given the
briefest of details. She didn't want Adam to think there was
anything between her and Carl, yet she couldn't tell him
the truth—that it was he she loved, that no other man would
do—and yet she couldn't hurt Carl either.

Adam continued to stand and stare and at length he said:
'Oh, I came to see Kenny.' Joanna stood up. 'No, I can see
him by myself.' From the window she watched him go with
the quick easy strides which everyone knew him by. He had
a flounce, she thought. An arrogant, bossy, distinguished
manner—but hell, she loved him just the same!

Joanna gave him time to talk to Kenny, then she casually
joined him to see other patients. It would be unbearable to
continue working alongside him, but he must never know
how much she was scarred inside. She must think only of
his wounded pride where Kamla was concerned.

Carl was waiting for Joanna when she went off duty and he
followed her to Willow-Weed Cottage where Kamla was
already preparing a meal. Joanna introduced them, and Carl
said at once how gorgeous the cottage was. Kamla had
prepared enough for three, so they ate a cosy meal, and
while they were sitting round the log fire drinking coffee
Kamla went to the hall to make a phone call. A short time
later she returned saying that she was going out, and it was
only after Adam had called to pick her up that Joanna
realised that she had been diplomatic in vacating the
cottage.

'Kamla felt embarrassed being with us. She didn't have to
go out, she gets very tired, we all do in our job. Now I feel
badly about it.'

'I appreciate it, though,' Carl said. 'After all, I won't be
here for many days and I would like you to myself as much
as possible.' He smiled warmly. 'Tomorrow I'll pick you up
and we'll have dinner at the Ploughman's Furrow.'

'But I shall have my car, I can meet you there.'

'I'd rather collect you myself.'

'I might get held up, Carl, so I'd prefer to be
independent,' Joanna insisted.

It was in the middle of the night when Joanna realised
what Carl was hoping would happen. He had a large room
at the Inn, he told her, where they could have a meal sent
up, but Joanna had other ideas, and when she went on duty
next day she found Lynn and said that she would like her

and Julian to meet her old friend at the Ploughman's
Furrow at eight o'clock, so that they could all have a drink
together. In spite of the day's busy schedule the time
seemed to drag, but at last Joanna went to the locker room
to change out of her uniform. It had been quite a pleasant
day, warm and sunny for late October, but by evening there
was a definite wintry chill in the air, so she had brought a
pleated skirt and light jumper to change into and was soon
off to the Inn, where she parked in one of the front spaces.
Carl was waiting outside to greet her.

'You could park round the back if you like?' he suggested,
but she smiled knowingly in the darkness and locked up her
car as if she hadn't heard. They went inside and at once he
offered her a drink which the barman brought over to their
table, and shortly afterwards Julian and Lynn walked in.
They looked around and waved in Joanna's direction before
picking up their drinks and coming over. Joanna introduced
them.

'Carl, you must remember Julian—Dr West from
Reading Hospital?'

Julian shook hands with Carl and both men appraised
each other suspiciously.

'Yes, I do vaguely remember you,' Julian said. 'But I was
a very junior houseman at the time.'

'You could hardly not recall that night,' Carl said, 'but
I'm afraid I've tried to shut out names and faces from
Reading. Fortunately my parents were in a position to have
me moved to London and a special clinic where I had all my
grafts done, but sadly it meant that Joanna and I lost touch
until recently.'

'Have you come for a meal or just a drink?' Joanna asked,
knowing full well what instructions she had given Lynn.

'I thought we'd eat here for a change, how about you?'
Julian asked.

'I've already ordered,' Carl said, and then another person
joined them and Joanna's face fell as she saw Adam waiting
to be introduced. He squeezed into the long settee under
the window next to Joanna so that he was constantly in the
conversation, and he too decided to eat with them, so any

idea Carl had of a romantic tête-à-tête in his room had to be abandoned. Joanna was aware of Adam's nearness, aware of his silent assessment of Carl, and all too aware of his attempt to steal Joanna's attention. She couldn't imagine what his game was. He couldn't care who her friends were or who she had dinner with, and what did Julian or Lynn think they were up to by including him when her plot was supposed to have been in confidence?

They had all been served with huge joints of succulent chicken in a basket, with large helpings of peas and chips, when Adam suddenly said:

'I've got just the thing for you, Joanna. A walkie-talkie effort so that you can get through to me at any time in case your car lets you down.'

'It's not that bad,' she protested. 'I do have it serviced regularly.'

'Well, I shall be much happier if I know you can contact me if you need me.'

Julian made a joke about her car and the conversation drifted merrily along over Joanna's head. Damn him, she thought angrily, I will marry Carl just to spite him! He's trying to put me down in front of Carl, showing up my weak points so that Carl will lose interest. Little do you know, she thought, Carl and I know one another very well, and maybe we deserve each other. When the landlord called for last orders everyone was in a frivolous mood except Joanna. It would have gone smoothly if Adam hadn't turned up, and now here he was ordering her to take this wretched walkie-talkie thing and insisting that he would follow her home. Carl looked slightly perplexed yet amused too. He walked to Joanna's car and bent to kiss her. 'See you tomorrow—but without the back-up troops, please,' he whispered.

'I didn't know they were coming to the same place for a meal,' she insisted, hoping she'd be forgiven for the little deception which, had Carl known had backfired somewhat. 'The Ploughman's Furrow is a favourite haunt of the staff at Ampfield.' She strapped herself in her beetle and followed Julian through the lanes, annoyed to think that Adam was behind her. Thank goodness it was too dark to see him in her mirror and once Julian had continued along the main road Joanna turned into the lane which led to the cottage. When she pulled into the drive he was right there with her and she accosted him angrily.

'I'm not a baby,' she said. 'I'm home now, so you can go on to Portia House.' To her dismay he got out of the car and with a very firm hand on her shoulder turned her towards the front door.

'Coffee,' he said shortly.

'It's too late to drink coffee.'

'Don't be so rude to your guests.'

She pushed open the door and walked angrily into the kitchen. Adam followed and closed the door after him.

'Don't shut that,' she commanded. 'We never shut the kitchen door.'

'We don't want to wake Kamla, do we?'

'Why didn't you stay here and keep her company, seeing that you think she's in some sort of danger here alone?'

'I was intrigued to meet your friend, Joanna, and to make sure you don't make the biggest mistake of your life.'

'What are you talking about?' In spite of not wanting coffee Joanna put the percolator on as she felt she was definitely going to need some stimulation.

Adam turned her round to face him and he held her arms painfully tightly. 'Pity is no substitute for love, Joanna. You know you don't love Carl, though I'm sure he's a very nice man.'

'How dare you!' Joanna spat indignantly, trying to tear herself free. 'How dare you interfere in my life! I don't know who told you where we were going tonight, but it was a private party.'

'Very private—and he had you already destined to share his room. It was just as well I did pop in for a drink.'

'Pop in for a drink!' Joanna scorned. 'I suppose Julian or Kamla told you where I was going and with whom.'

'Kamla would have come too, but she was on call. I wanted to give you this walkie-talkie and she happened to mention where Carl was staying and that you were meeting him at the Inn.'

'Well, you can take your silly walkie-talkie away with you. I don't need your help, Adam. I've been living here for over three years perfectly all right without anyone's protection.'

'Not quite. There used to be Julian.'

'So?'

'So, because he's attached to Lynn now you need someone—but you didn't have to go to London and look up old boyfriends.'

'You are despicable!' she shouted, and at that moment the coffee bubbled noisily, spilling over on to the stove.

With a sigh of irritation she fetched a cloth and mopped it up, then waited for it to brew the required eight minutes, during which Adam leaned against the worktop watching her with amused interest.

'Just because you were involved in the same accident and both sustained similar injuries it doesn't mean you have to marry the man, Joanna. You only think you could make a go of it because you've suffered together.'

'And who said anything about marriage?' She turned on him aggressively. 'Can't I meet an old friend without creating such animosity—and what's it to you anyway?'

She poured coffee into two mugs, added cold milk—an indication that she didn't expect him to stay longer than was necesssary—and pushed his along the worktop, trying to avoid meeting his stern gaze.'

'Your welfare is everything to me, Joanna, as I've told you before. Remember, I know what you're capable of and I don't want to see you throwing yourself away on any man who'll have you.'

'You . . . you . . .' she pursed her lips together angrily, searching for the right words, words which would hurt him as much as he was hurting her. 'You only know what I'm capable of because you used me,' she accused. 'If anyone needs to be reminded that pity is no substitute for love it's you!'

The air was filled with dissension. Joanna couldn't bear to look at Adam—she didn't need to as she could feel his thirst for retaliation—but he drank his coffee down and with a murmured goodnight left Willow-Weed.

Joanna knew she had touched a raw nerve, but it wouldn't hurt him to be told the truth. He had only made love to her because he felt sorry for her, and to keep her away from her home while Kamla and Das sorted out their problems, and in the sorting they had given Adam a bigger problem if he was genuinely in love with Kamla himself. That was what hurt, Joanna realised painfully. She could have borne his pity because she loved him so much, but to have used her when Kamla had decided to honour her parents' wishes was too much to bear. Joanna wanted him, she would always crave for his love—but not on those terms.

CHAPTER TWELVE

JOANNA'S heart ached miserably, not only with love for Adam but because she knew that he was right about Carl. It might be unrequited love, it was also guilt and pity combined, but she couldn't help the feeling that she owed Carl something—her very life, possibly. Now she was guilty too of leading him on, letting him think there might be a chance for them to make a go of marriage for whatever reason. She felt trapped. After that one night of ecstasy with Adam she realised that she was undermining her own sexual drive if she imagined she could go through life without a man's love. But who was there who would truly love her? With Julian it had been familiarity, a growing together through circumstances, and marriages had been based on far less and proved successful, she told herself. But now he had found true love, not just mutual respect, mutual admiration, but a deep and lasting devotion which both he and Lynn shared. Joanna might have felt jealous if she were the type to covet over people's happiness, but all she wanted was to be able to show her feelings for Adam. By the contemptuous way he looked at her now, though, she knew she had ended even a compatible friendship.

Carl stayed on for three more days during which they met up, dined out, visited the Cathedral and shopping centre at Tullbury, but on his last evening he came to Willow-Weed for supper. Kamla was not at home, whether by design or accident Joanna didn't know, but she almost wished the Indian doctor would return. Somehow Joanna knew that she had to let Carl down lightly. It wouldn't be fair to let him return to London with hope when she knew that nothing could come of their relationship. She wished she could condition herself to feel differently, but the more she was with Carl the more positive she was of the changes the years had made. Carl laughed at himself a great deal, but it covered up the deep emotional scar which no one could heal. They laughed together, held meaningful discussions about life and its complexes, but there was no excitement, no urgent desire to become intimate which should precede any consideration of holy matrimony. That marriage was a sacred status was becoming clearer to Joanna as thoughts of happiness slipped from her grasp, but with Carl there could be no violation of the truth.

The log fire burned with yellow flames, an occasional spit and a delicious aroma of tar and resin as they sat on the settee sipping the remainder of the superb mature wine which Carl had brought, and chatting about old times.

After a lull Carl shifted uneasily in his place and Joanna recognised the signs of a delicate subject about to be broached.

'It's been a lovely break for me here,' he said with an emotional crack in his voice. 'I won't repeat my proposal of marriage because I understand how things are here. Well, partly—I can't be sure whether you're pining over Julian or whether the Godfather is the man who's causing you so much anguish.'

Joanna felt a rush of blood to her cheeks as she looked across at him, her eyes wide in astonishment.

'Come on, Joey. Too much water under the bridge to hedge any more, and if you were thinking of marrying me out of pity, or guilt, then forget it. I have to confess that I'd never given you much thought over the years, but then I wouldn't—there was too much healing to be done—but seeing you at the buffet on the station with your aunts, so much of my anguish fell away. I put on a good act—well, I try to for my parents' sakes, but there's a hell of a lot of pain inside which I suppose will never go away. I guess I was clutching at straws from the past, Joey. If there'd been any real love between us we wouldn't have let the years pass by without communicating, would we?'

'I often thought about you,' she admitted gently. 'I naturally blamed myself for you being so badly burned—

and after all that we lost Emma. We both needed rehabilitation treatment to get over the shock. There's so much more to "shock" than people realise. It goes deep and ravages, and only kindness helps to heal it. At least you had your parents. Mine came and went again within weeks. Julian became my prop, and it's only recently that I've realised that what I felt for him wasn't true love.'

'So it's Adam? He's the Godfather?' Carl smiled. 'Walkie-talkie, seeing you home, getting you to take Kamla as a paying guest? What makes you think he's doing all these things for anything but love, Joey?'

'Love for Kamla!' Joanna sneered. 'I feel sorry for him that she changed her mind about marrying Das, but I do see that they became genuinely fond of each other. It's only natural, after all, though I know mixed marriages can work exceedingly well.' She laughed mockingly. 'Kamla has been using Adam.'

Carl only raised his eyebrows and then with a groan stood up. 'Too much good food and wine, and I'm getting lazy, so it's off to the Continent tomorrow or the day after. I wish things could have worked out for us, Joey, but I understand.'

After he had gone Joanna went to bed and wept tears of sorrow for him. She didn't think she had ever felt quite so alone in all her life.

Adam went about his duties with a permanent scowl on his face, so much so that the staff began to talk and speculate as to the reason for his ill-temper. He spoke to Joanna only when it was absolutely necessary concerning their patients, and Joanna found the situation intolerable. She toyed with the idea of going away for a longer holiday—yes, she thought, even to see her parents—but as quickly shelved that idea. Perhaps it was time to change jobs. Go to a hospital miles away and work in general surgery—anything, anywhere as long as she could get out of this cruel rut. She found it difficult to concentrate when Adam came to do his next round, but in the middle of it he was paged to answer the telephone. An urgent call, the switchboard operator said, but after twenty minutes he was back wearing a puzzled frown, and as the days went by he seemed to come out of his depression, so that at least they were able to revert to their previous level of tolerating each other for the sake of their patients.

The much dreaded Guy Fawkes Night arrived, when all the staff prayed for wet weather, but it was clear and bright with a myriad stars illuminating the sky, no need for extra fireworks, Joanna thought. She went home for a meal late afternoon, as everyone available was requested to be on duty, call or standby hoping against hope that the public would be sensible and attend properly organised display functions rather than private Bonfire Night parties which could so easily get out of hand. She stood at the window in one of the corridors on the first floor and watched the glow of bonfires on the horizon, and rockets shooting up in the air, letting out screams and wails as they fell to the ground. Then a different sound echoed through the air, the ominous sound of an ambulance siren, so she went along to the lift and down to the accident and emergency area where Adam, Julian, Kamla, Lynn and a team of other nurses were all standing by.

'I may as well come down to join you. We've got three empty beds and can probably make room for two or three more makeshift if necessary, but please God, they won't be,' she said quietly to Lynn.

'Last year, after all the publicity the media put out, we only had three casualties and none of them serious. Let's hope this year will be no worse, but we've already had a man in who was walking about stoking up his bonfire with his jacket on fire. Men are worse than little boys, you'd expect them to know better,' Lynn grumbled.

'I used to quite like the excitement of Bonfire Night,' Joanna admitted. 'Sparklers and hot soup, even my brother chasing me with jumping jacks and grasshoppers, but not any more. I don't mind the big displays properly organised, but bonfires can soon get out of control. I wonder who this is?' Joanna said, turning round as the ambulance men came in with a stretcher case.

'It would help if you could take the particulars from the relatives, Joanna, while I assist Adam.'

Distraught parents were reluctant to leave the side of their teenage daughter, but Adam had to insist so that he could get on with the job of assessing and treating her.

Joanna took them into a small cubicle and sat them down.

'We'll get you a cup of tea in a moment,' she said gently, 'but first we'd like some particulars please. Her name, address and date of birth?'

'Sally . . . Sally Turner,' the father said, and after Joanna had written down all the relevant details she asked a junior nurse to go for a tray of tea. Sally was just fifteen and her party had been a combined bonfire and birthday one as it usually was.

'Stupid youngsters,' Mr Turner complained. 'I said no more than ten, but more and more kids turned up—with drink too—something we don't allow as yet. Eighteen is soon enough, in my opinion. Trouble is they can get it from supermarkets all too easily and I reckon they were well hyped up before they ever got to Sally's party.'

Mrs Turner was trembling with fear, but she laid a hand on her husband's arm. 'Bill dear, Sister isn't interested in what we think. It's too late for recriminations now. One of the lads must have thrown an empty beer can on to the fire and it exploded. Sally was bent down trying to light a sparkler for her younger sister. She's badly hurt, her face is all burnt up. She might lose her sight . . .'

Joanna talked and consoled, plied them with tea and prayed a silent prayer for Sally. She went through to the treatment room to make enquiries, and as she stood looking down at the pathetic figure on the trolley her brain spun with memories of screaming; she could smell the smoke and hear the roof timbers falling . . . falling . . .

'It's all right, Joey,' Julian whispered. 'She'll be all right—just as you were.' He guided her through to another empty room and sat her down. 'Head between your knees, deep breaths . . . good girl . . .'

Dear Julian, always there—what would she do without him!

Much later when Sally had been admitted to Intensive Care Joanna sat with her monitoring her condition and chatting. The parents, who had two younger children, had been assured that Sally was in capable hands and had been persuaded to return home so that Sally could rest. Joanna knew that grafts would be required after the initial shock and burnt skin had been dealt with, but for now Sally needed quiet sympathy and understanding.

The midnight hour passed and it was well past one o'clock when Sally began weeping and talking fast.

'I'm burning—my face—my hair—Mum! Mum!' she screeched.

'It's all right, dear,' Joanna whispered, holding the girl's hands firmly. 'You're safe now, just lie still and rest.'

'I can't see—I'm blind—my eyes aren't there any more—I'm burning up . . .'

'You're in shock, Sally. It's all over now, try to relax . . . open your eyes, you can see me, I'm sure.'

Joanna knew that her eyelids and face would feel stiff, but she persuaded her to open her eyes gradually and was ready with a compassionate smile when she did. Gradually Joanna explained about her injuries. 'Time is the magic healer,' she said, and as the minutes ticked by she found herself telling Sally about her own accident. 'It's marvellous what the doctors can do, and in time no one will ever know what happened, Sally. It's all a question of patience, and co-operating with the medical staff. Everyone is here to help you. I'm going to get the doctor to write up for something to help you relax.' Joanna stood up, and bumped into a masculine figure.

'It's all right, Joanna, I'm here,' Adam said kindly. 'Night Sister has the injection prepared and is coming to take over. You must get home—there's another day tomorrow. The worst is over, parties aren't likely to last after two o'clock. Go and get yourself a cup of tea first. We've done pretty well this year. No really serious cases, Sally will look as good as new again, and she's young—and with your persuasive charm to urge her to fight she'll make it. Julian and Lynn are going to stay on.'

Joanna felt a lump rise in her throat. They were colleagues working for the benefit of people in trouble, that was one thing they could agree on, but oh, how mentally exhausted she felt! She wanted to get home, to be alone, yet as she fastened her seat-belt in her old beetle she couldn't move as the dark night seemed to taunt her with old memories. Why had they returned so vividly all of a sudden? She thought she had managed to lay the ghost of the fire as the years had slipped by. Was it seeing Carl again? It was like being in a time machine, so vivid were the pictures of the dance hall and the hospital in Reading. She wept silently as she sat alone in the dark, and then with sudden verve she started up the engine, dabbed her eyes again, and set the wheels in motion. She was suffering from delayed reaction, she supposed. Excitement, enthusiasm at seeing Carl again had opened up a whole new avenue of thoughts, but now she must settle back to work and forget the past. There was Sally to help, and no matter how much heartache she was experiencing she must put her patients before herself. Halfway up the hill the engine began to splutter.

'Come on,' she said hopefully. 'This isn't the time and place to let me down.' The light of the bright moon reflected on something shiny lying on her passenger seat and she managed to smile at the sight of her walkie-talkie set. She made the hill with a struggle and as she turned down the quiet lane and levelled off the car ran more easily, and then Joanna heard some crackling.

'Calling Beetle—over!'

The voice made her start. She hadn't used this contraption—not even paid attention when Adam had tried to explain how it worked, much less left it switched on. A trick. Carl! Was he lurking still in the vicinity? She felt a moment's relaxation at the thought, then panic—no, she didn't want to see him again. It was over, they had both survived, but there was still time for a new life to begin for each of them.

'Well, answer the damned thing, Joanna!' Now there was

no mistaking Adam's voice.

She managed to pick it up and control the car at the same time.

'Are you trying to get me killed?' she demanded angrily. 'I didn't switch the thing on, and I'm nearly home now.'

'I know that. I switched it on in readiness, knowing how contrary you can be. It's lonely and dark, and—and—I just wanted to say, I love you!'

Joanna applied her brakes and stopped before she did herself a mischief.

'You're trying to finish me off.' She couldn't have heard right. He was teasing her, trying to antagonise her—no, she wouldn't rise to his bait. 'I don't know what you think you're doing,' she went on testily, 'but I want to get home to bed.'

There was a long pause, then a seductive chuckle. It just wasn't fair that he had such a deep brown voice that made her knees turn to jelly.

'So do I—so do I.' Another mischievous laugh. 'Darling, don't you know you should say 'over and out', and all that stuff?'

'It ought to be illegal to speak on these things when you're driving along.'

'But you're not driving—you've stopped. I can't hear the engine.'

If Joanna has been standing she would have stamped her foot angrily. 'Oh, you . . . you . . .'

'I love you, Joanna. I'm parked in a farm gateway a hundred feet from where you've stopped. I've been waiting and worrying. What took you so long?'

'Adam . . .' She could barely breathe his name. He had said he loved her and it sounded as if he meant it. 'Couldn't I go on home?'

'Of course. What are we waiting for?—though I must confess I thought this idea was rather romantic.'

'I never thought of you as being romantic,' Joanna said softly.

'You've been too busy trying to read all kinds of nonsensical messages into other people's affairs. I like

Kamla very much indeed, but anything I've done for her has been because I felt sorry for her in that particular situation. It's true I had to scheme a bit to get Julian off your back, but I could see Lynn was tearing herself apart with envy, and it worked—they don't call me Godfather for nothing.'

'Adam how did you know how I felt about you?' she asked tremulously.

'I thought we made love because we truly loved each other,' he said. 'I don't do that kind of thing unless it means something special, but then I thought you hated me, but Carl is no fool, is he?'

'What's Carl got to do with it?' she asked curtly.

'He telephoned me after he'd left, and realised that he didn't stand a chance with you. He said he wasn't certain whether it was Julian or me until you'd talked, and he guessed that you'd never be brave enough to tell me yourself. Pride and all that too—you are a silly girl—but I reckon that seeing him again has finally made you realise that life has to go on, Joanna. You can't retain the hurt, you must let the past go, my darling.'

Joanna buried her face in her handkerchief and sobbed. The walkie-talkie crackled by her side as she replaced it on the seat, and then a gentle tap on the window made her jump.

Adam opened the door and pulled her to her feet, enclosing her in his arms, kissing her with the passion she remembered from their one night of love.

'Love knows no bounds, my sweet,' he said ardently. 'Love conquers, love heals—love is the cure.'

Joanna gave herself up to him, the past dead and buried, a new beginning with a love so tender, so divine that already her vision was dancing with bells and orange-blossom and scars that were fading fast.

'You can get rid of that old walkie-talkie,' she said.

'Not on your life! I want to be able to tell you much I love you at any time of the night or day—and I want you to be able to tell me——'

'I love you, Adam, I truly love you—for healing the scars of my heart.'

This Christmas Temptation Is Irresistible

Our scintillating selection makes an ideal Christmas gift. These four new novels by popular authors are only available in this gift pack. They're tempting, sensual romances created especially to satisfy the desires of today's woman and at this fantastic price you can even treat yourself!

CARDINAL RULES – *Barbara Delinsky*
A WEDDING GIFT – *Kristin James*
SUMMER WINE – *Ethel Paquin*
HOME FIRES – *Candace Schuler*

Give in to Temptation this Christmas.
Available November 1988 Price: £5.00

Doctor Nurse Romances

Romance in modern medical life

Read more about the lives and loves of doctors and nurses in the fascinatingly different backgrounds of contemporary medicine. These are the three Doctor Nurse romances to look out for next month.

MIRACLES TAKE LONGER
Sarah Franklin

THE DOCTORS AT ST ANNE'S
Sheila Douglas

SURGEON ROYAL
Margaret Barker

Buy them from your usual paperback stockist, or write to: Mills & Boon Reader Service, P.O. Box 236, Thornton Rd, Croydon, Surrey CR9 3RU, England. Readers in Southern Africa — write to: Independent Book Services Pty, Postbag X3010, Randburg, 2125, S. Africa.

Mills & Boon
the rose of romance

THREE TOP AUTHORS.
THREE TOP STORIES.

TWILIGHT WHISPERS — *Barbara Delinsky* — £3.50
Another superb novel from Barbara Delinsky, author of 'Within Reach' and 'Finger Prints.' This intense saga is the story of the beautiful Katia Morell, caught up in a whirlwind of power, tragedy, love and intrigue.

INTO THE LIGHT — *Judith Duncan* — £2.50
The seeds of passion sown long ago have borne bitter fruit for Natalie. Can Adam forget his resentment and forgive her for leaving, in this frank and compelling novel of emotional tension and turmoil.

AN UNEXPECTED PLEASURE — *Nancy Martin* — £2.25
A top journalist is captured by rebels in Central America and his colleague and lover follows him into the same trap. Reality blends with danger and romance in this dramatic new novel.

Available November 1988

W🌐RLDWIDE

Available from Boots, Martins, John Menzies, W.H. Smith,
Woolworths and other paperback stockists.